Praise for

Theory & Practice

WINNER OF THE STELLA PRIZE

A *NEW YORK TIMES BOOK REVIEW* EDITORS' CHOICE

'The excesses of 1980s academia are ripe fodder for De Kretser's mordant wit, but her aim here is more ambitious—and the results more rewarding . . . A bold experiment in form . . . A taut, enthralling hybrid of fact and fiction.'

EMILY EAKIN, *The New York Times Book Review*

'A curious book, an ambiguous mixture of nostalgia and satire, and of fiction and memoir . . . De Kretser, a sharp, nimble stylist, seeds in charming flashes of dry humor throughout.'

SAM SACKS, *The Wall Street Journal*

'A Sally Rooney–ish, political/feminist picaresque, whose fiercely truth-seeking narrator both acts within and reports upon the shape-shifting social and academic organisms she's part of . . . De Kretser's writing is unfailingly smart . . . Fearless lines zap every page.'

JOAN FRANK, *The Washington Post*

'In many ways, *Theory & Practice* is like a coming-of-age novel or perhaps a coming-to-writing novel, and

De Kretser is a beautifully sly writer . . . As De Kretser shows us from its very beginning, *Theory & Practice* is anything but conventional. It is something new, born of the recognition between holding two truths in mind at once.'
JESSICA FERRI, *Los Angeles Times*

'A slim novel that manages to be both intellectually thrilling and stunningly intimate. A warm and funny read by one of Australia's finest writers.'
KATE TUTTLE, *The Boston Globe*

'*Theory & Practice* is sly, spiky, and brilliant: an intellectual coming-of-age story that accounts for all that can't be learned in the academy—or in books . . . [It] flits confidently between modes: memoir and novel, personal and political, fact and fiction. Essayistic asides commingle with tender memories; heady emotions intrude on serious philosophizing. The aim, the narrator says, is to capture a sense of 'formlessness and mess'—in other words, real life.'
SOPHIA STEWART, *The Atlantic*

'This appears to be De Kretser's impetus: to tread where Woolf refrained, to push the margins of what a novel can look and feel like. It also asks questions of the act of reading itself . . . This is a book of intrusions: of unacknowledged inequalities, of flawed maternal figures, of raw human emotions (our "morbid symptoms") . . . So much is condensed into its brief length, not least of which is a probing interrogation of novels and why we write them . . . As De Kretser accomplishes in *Theory & Practice*, they allow witness of life's "messy, human truth," told without shame.'

JACK CALLIL, *The Guardian*

'[De Kretser] has blown the doors off completely . . . *Theory & Practice* has something for everyone. It is a book that revels in the complexity of real life, the messy practice of things that theory tries to smooth over . . . It's just a damned good book.'

JOHN SELF, *The Times* (London)

'An evocative, shifting novel of time and place . . . De Kretser [is] alive throughout this ever-inventive novel to the urgent necessities of desire and their unforeseen consequences. Her ending returns you to her beginning, to the mythical-seeming story of the boy in the outback throwing all that glitters into oblivion; to the false start that leads to her latest quest for fictional truth. It is a measure of De Kretser's beguiling talent as a novelist that she holds both these tales in balance without the whole ever threatening to fall apart.'

TIM ADAMS, *The Observer* (UK)

'An exceptional novelist—perhaps among the ten best at work in English today . . . An innovative, compelling book which takes ingenious steps to persuade us that we are not reading fiction but documentary truth . . . Like De Kretser's other work, *Theory & Practice* is a novel of considerable wit and brutal comedy . . . Humour in De Kretser is a sign of keen understanding and intelligence. She is writing about something of significance, but a novelist of this grace, linguistic bravura and inventiveness could write about nothing of significance and still hold our attention and admiration . . . This is an author working at the top of her game.'

PHILIP HENSHER, *The Spectator*

'De Kretser is one of the most quietly thrilling writers around—so sharp, funny and inventive that I can only envy anyone who hasn't had the joy of reading her . . . The winningly candid protagonist is delicious company.' ANTHONY CUMMINS, *The Daily Mail*

'De Kretser's seventh novel . . . follow[s] the experience of the narrator, a young Sri Lankan Australian woman, as she attends graduate school in Melbourne. While working on a thesis about Virginia Woolf, she considers what it means to be a "modern woman" in an intellectual milieu saturated with French theory. Drawn into an affair with another student, she grapples with her feminism and discovers unexpected points of contact between ideas and physical passion.'

The New Yorker

‘Startlingly intelligent and stylish.’

JASMINE VOJDANI, *New York*

‘A complex, lyrical story of relationships, feminism, and academic pressure.’ *People*

Theory

& Practice

ALSO BY MICHELLE DE KRETSER

The Rose Grower
The Hamilton Case
The Lost Dog
Questions of Travel
Springtime
The Life to Come
On Shirley Hazzard
Scary Monsters

Theory & Practice

A Novel

Michelle de Kretser

Catapult New York

THEORY & PRACTICE

First Catapult edition: 2025
First paperback edition: 2026

Hardcover ISBN: 978-1-64622-287-2
Paperback ISBN: 978-1-64622-322-0

Library of Congress Control Number: 2024947932

Cover design by Jaya Miceli
Cover images: Virginia Woolf © George C. Beresford / Wikipedia: Public Domain; floral pattern © Shutterstock / Lera Eframova
Book design by Wah-Ming Chang

Catapult
New York, NY
books.catapult.co

Printed in the United States of America

1 3 5 7 9 10 8 6 4 2

for the Maternal line

My mother told me, *they'll want you to tell them your story*, the girl said. My mother said, *don't. You are not anyone's story.*

ALI SMITH, *Spring*

This is where I came from.
I passed this way.
This should not be shameful
Or hard to say.

JAMES FENTON, 'The Ideal'

Theory

& Practice

At first he barely notices the children. They're waiting for the bus, a small boy, and a girl of about ten with braided hair. He's twenty-three, too close to childhood and too far from it to find children of consequence. Also, a Spanish music teacher in London is keeping him from thinking about anyone else. She'd sent him a letter *poste restante* that reached him in France. The letter was friendly and calm. A day later he had it by heart. In Switzerland he's still running his mind over it, hunting. He's searching for the chain of requests, expectations, and subtle demands with which he believes women make prisoners of men.

It's 1957. Back in Australia, rivers of southern Europeans are pouring into Sydney from ships docked at Circular Quay. They flood the city with superstitions, politics, emotions, smells. They draw attention to themselves with noisy colours. He met the music teacher twice, and twice she was wearing a flowery red shirt. A bracelet, a band of blue, showed where a cuff met a wrist. The wrist was thick and looked strong – he's seen the same peasant hands gripping suitcases in newsreels. The impression of strength runs contrary to his idea of a female musician, which is based on an engraving of the young Clara Schumann that hangs in the institution where his mother is housed.

The music teacher brought up politics at once, informing him that her family had fled Barcelona at the end of the civil war. That means her people must be communists, so why begin her letter with a hand-drawn cross? Another thing is that she has blue eyes and fair hair, although Spaniards are dark. Her contradictions excite and unsettle him. Are they symptoms of Old World sophistication or European deceit?

Most disturbing of all is his sense that she knows everything he thinks about her and is amused by it.

What cause does a Spanish music teacher have to be amused by an Australian geologist?

The Swiss children stand near him but apart, absorbed in a clapping game. When their voices finally catch his attention, he can't follow the words of their chant. His French is scanty, scraped up from memories of school and the month he's just spent in France. The chant begins with an exclamation – *O bella!* – as the children clap palms. As the quick-fire ritual goes on, the boy has trouble keeping up. Whenever he gets it wrong, the game stops and his sister drills him. There's one unmistakeable meaning, a finger drawn across the throat and the cry, *Tu es mort!*

The children choose the seat across from him on the bus. The girl pulls an exercise book from her bag and turns to a page near the back. She reads from it under her breath, and he realises that she's rehearsing the chant. She interrupts herself to touch her brother's cheek, under his eye. She holds out her forefinger, and the boy leans forward, purses his lips, closes his eyes, and blows on the lash to make a wish. Then he lies down and places his head in her lap. Halfway up the mountain, the two of them leave the bus.

His stop is the last one, a village where he rents a cheap attic room. Seven glorious days follow. He clambers over black rocks at the foot of a glacier lifted from a textbook. He whistles 'The Happy Wanderer' while following a forest path. He confirms that La Dent Blanche means 'the white tooth' – it's the name of a mountain. He lies on his back in an alpine meadow where sleek, hefty cows are pastured for summer. He eats a slab of cow, sitting on a terrace in iris-blue dusk. He sleeps with his quilt pulled over his head because the church bell sounds the hour all through the night. He wakes in the chilly morning to the sight of the White Tooth. The day – no, light itself – seems to flow from that mountain. It's preposterous how reliably Switzerland looks like Switzerland: chalets, cows, ice-blue lakes, hillsides of coloured flowers. One day a man goes past with an alpenhorn the length of the village street. Larches green the slopes, row upon regimental row. The clouds move swiftly, and so do the streams. What he'd noticed first in Europe was its filth – grimy London! grubby Paris! His aunt in

Twickenham stored books in her bath! But Switzerland shines: the air, the peaks, the apple-fleshed people, the glasses in the restaurant where he drinks too much schnapps on his last night in the Alps.

He blames the schnapps for summoning the dream, which has been calling on him for years. It shows him a group of little girls in identical dresses on a lawn. They're tramping around in a circle, their hands linked in a game. In the background stands a large Edwardian house with verandahs and gables. He watches the scene from the gate. A child with springy, side-parted hair senses his presence and smiles at him over her shoulder. That's when he wakes up.

Aged six, he spent two months on a sheep station in New South Wales. Those months are a sequence of jerky images, scratched, fading at the edges like an old, faulty film. His father was at the war, his mother fell ill, and he was sent to his father's parents. He was told that they'd visited Sydney before the war, but he had no clear picture of them. He arrived with a box of soldiers and a cough. His grandmother propped him on a sofa, buttressed him with cushions, and brought him a drink made with blackcurrant jam. Her hands were as white and soft as flowers. They were also knobbly with rings.

His grandmother was like that, both yielding and

hard. The maids went about the house with careful faces. Very soon – a small, puzzling discovery – he realised that she didn't like his mother. Screened by a wingback armchair, he heard her say, 'He looks so much like Bessie. I do hope he doesn't have her nerves.'

Days were yellow in the middle.

Days were mud, paddocks, kelpies, sheep.

Days were helping Jack stir molasses into the feed for the rams.

Days were lemonade scones.

Days were weather.

All at once he understood 'horizon'. It was *there* – an astonishment.

He helped his grandmother parcel up the socks she'd knitted for the troops and the scarf she was sending his father. She listened to his reading. She read to him, sitting by his high iron bed. They played backgammon when it rained. He had trouble with his laces, so she showed him a way that began with two loops.

All the way to the gate, past the leafless elms and on to the dam, he sat in front of his grandmother on her horse. She was pillowy, lovely to lean against, but he sat up straight as instructed. There'd be a pony of his own if he was still there at Christmas, his grandmother whispered. Her large, veined hands were nothing like his mother's, which were small and had bitten nails. He loved his grandmother's hands, busy with rings and reins.

She kept most of her rings on her dressing table, but the best ring lived in the morning room in a glass-lidded box that was locked. He liked to lean over the lid, studying the contents of the box: medals, a belt, a pair of binoculars, a silver cigarette case, a silver matchbox cover, and the ring. All these things had belonged to Great-Uncle Jocelyn, killed in France in a different war. His grandmother unlocked the box and handed him the ring. It had been made from the fuse cap of a spent German shell, she said. A difficult word thickened his tongue: 'aluminium'. The tip of his grandmother's finger touched the flower carved on the ring. 'Jocelyn chose a daisy because my name's Margaret. *Marguerite* is French for "daisy". He made the ring for me.'

'Why don't you wear it?' It lay on his palm. He thought it far more important than all her other rings. 'It's beautiful.'

'Do you think so?'

'Is it worth a lot of money?'

'It's the most precious thing I own.'

Without warning, it was spring. A letter brought the news that his mother was well. He was to go home at the end of the week. His mother enclosed a note for him with a drawing of the tree outside her window. She was longing to see him, she wrote; he must have grown as tall as a tree.

It was a day full of wind. The hedge was alive with fresh red leaves. He felt like those leaves: tossed and changed. His mother was silly – no one was as tall as a tree! He wanted his silly mother and he wanted a pony. He took a ring with three green stones from his grandmother's room. He did it quickly, so that he wasn't really taking it. The grown-up world lobbed him here and there and never asked for his consent. Now there would be no pony, although he'd already chosen its name.

Never again would the sky be as enormous. In a tussocky gully he squatted over a trail of ants with neither beginning nor end. He grazed his shin as he scrambled out. Magpies whistled. He took the ring with three green stones from his pocket. It winked at him – how stupid it was! He hurled it into a thicket of trees. He watched a ewe rubbing herself on a fence. He'd been looking forward to the shearing – that was another thing that wouldn't happen. He stood on a rock shouting, 'Bum! Bum! Bum!'

On his second-last morning, his grandmother missed her emerald ring. Maids took up rugs and crawled over the floor. Men parted leafy clumps and stooped. The wastepaper baskets were upended. His grandmother gave orders while turning out drawers. He searched too, lifting cushions, until his grandmother barked that he was getting in the way.

He returned to the thicket and searched.

In a paddock buzzy with flies, he sat cross-legged to think.

He thought all through lunch.

At tea time he thought while eating cake.

The ring with three green stones was lost.

It wasn't precious like the ring in the glass-lidded box.

So what use to say?

His grandmother spoke on the phone. 'We've searched very thoroughly, I assure you, even though it's quite impossible that it slipped from my finger. I have to use soap when I want to take it off.'

It was his last evening, so he had grown-up supper for a treat. Damask roses gleamed on the cloth. Candles towered in twisted sticks. Lace frothed at his grandmother's throat. Everything was different. His glass was apple green. His collar was itchy. With his back to the fire, he grew helplessly hot.

His grandfather had a spring, a summer, and half an autumn left to live. The boy's memory would wipe him almost completely away. There remained a red dog dashing to the old man's bellow, 'Blue!'; and the question, salvaged from dinner that night, 'Why Pearlie?'

Pearlie worked in the kitchen. He'd seen her scouring a pan.

'The others have been with us for years. She'll have buried it. Or hidden it in a tree. When the fuss dies down, one of the other natives will retrieve it. They stick together – you know how it is.' His grandmother added, 'She ought to be whipped.'

A great shiver ran through him. His spoon shuddered on his plate. The air around his grandmother went ripply. She inspected him, frothy and glittery over the candles. He steadied himself. He spooned up soup.

The next morning Jack carried his case out to the car and stored it in the boot. He was to be driven to the station and delivered to a conductor on a train. He remembered, hazily, that this had already happened to him once and was simply another thing to be endured.

He walked down the steps with his grandmother. She kissed him, wrapping him in softness. She slipped something hard into his hand.

On the long, flat road into town, a cloud of dust approached. 'Father Tully,' said Jack. 'Coming for Pearlie, ay.'

He said nothing. What was there to say? He was going to his mother with a soldier's ring and the knowledge that he didn't have her nerves.

It's the morning after the dream. He heaves his knapsack onto a bus. This one will take him down the mountain, where he'll catch a train to the St Bernard Pass. Pearlie was a big girl, thirteen or more. The girl in his dream is younger, more like the age he was back then. She's darker, too, than Pearlie, but he knows they're one and the same. He also knows that the house with the gables stands at a crossroads, although there are no roads in the dream.

The bus gathers in a tired-looking woman with a baby. He drags his mind from the past. Clouds are going about their work of changing the shadows on the mountains. One of the mountains is green with umber stripes running at a diagonal, larches and sandstone. Far below, he spots the emerald wedges of an alluvial fan. It tells him that a stream once flowed down an alp and spread itself out on the floor of the valley. He wonders if it still does, after rain.

The music teacher, having conceded a minor defeat to the scenery, sets about shoving mountains aside. She hurries into a room out of a spring shower, smoothing rain-darkened hair. He discovers a tenderness that complicates his breathing.

It's almost August. Leaving home in January, he'd planned to spend the whole year seeing Britain and the Continent. But what will it mean to go on to Italy? It'll be France all over again: heat, swindles, trains that don't arrive, olive oil to unsettle his stomach. On the other hand, there's Austria. He doesn't think 'schnitzel' and 'waltzes' and 'goosestepping', so horror doesn't twist up inside him. He's pressed a flower, a gentian, a witchy blue-black, for the music teacher. He'll buy a postcard, a stamp, and a beer while waiting for a train to Innsbruck or Graz. He'll write, 'I'll be returning to London in September.'

The baby's delighted face rises over the back of a seat: her mother lifts and lowers her, cooing. The bus slows – there's a village ahead. On the far side of the road he sees a fountain and a woodpile, and a shop with an awning where apricots are for sale. On the near side he sees the girl with the braids and her brother. The boy is sitting on the wall that borders the road, playing with a yo-yo. The girl has the same polished hair as the music teacher. She's stepping sideways along the wall in her sandals, her back to the dizzying drop. Are all Swiss children like that, sure-footed and fearless? He remembers three he saw in the mountains, racing one another down a plunging track.

The bus is level with the girl when a look of wonder comes over her face. He shouts. So does the woman with the baby. They shout uselessly, instinctively, and in two different languages: 'Stop!'

✦

At that point, the novel I was writing stalled.

✦

In December 2021, an essay called 'Tunnel Vision' by Eyal Weizman appeared in the *London Review of Books*. 'Tunnel Vision' read like fiction but recounted atrocious facts. Its subject was the Israeli military commander

Aviv Kochavi. At the Operational Theory Research Institute at Israel's National Defense College, Kochavi had encountered canonical works of poststructuralist and urban theory, including Situationist texts.

In 2002, Kochavi led a raid into the West Bank city of Nablus, and Balata, an adjoining refugee camp. He directed his soldiers away from streets and alleys, where they would be vulnerable to snipers. Instead, the Israelis crossed the territory through its buildings, battering holes in party walls and taking the Palestinian resistance by surprise.

A Palestinian woman called Aisha asks us to imagine the scene. We're sitting in our living room with our family. Suddenly part of a wall disappears in a roar, there's dust and debris everywhere, and soldiers shouting orders stream into the room through the hole. Their faces are painted black, they're in full battle gear, and their machine guns are trained on us. Our children scream and scream. Are the soldiers coming for us? Or does our house merely lie on their way to somewhere else? The answer comes when they smash a hole in another wall and move on to our neighbour's place.

According to Weizman, Kochavi attributed the success of the raid to his reinterpretation of space. He called it 'walking through walls' and 'adjusting' the relevant urban space to his 'needs'. Weizman suggests that Kochavi's strategy was inspired by the key Situationist concepts of *dérive* and *détournement*. The first refers to unhindered movement through a city without regard for 'borders'; the second to the adaptation of buildings for new ends.

The tunnel strategy forced Palestinian fighters to abandon buildings for the streets, where they were easily hunted down. When they asked to surrender, Kochavi refused. The purpose of the raid was to kill as many people as possible in a short time before withdrawing.

Seventy Palestinians were killed by the Israeli Defense Forces in the attack on Nablus and Balata that day. The tunnel strategy went on to be copied by militaries around the world.

In the weeks after I read about Kochavi's application of Situationist theory to colonising practice, experiences I'd had, over time, with theory and practice kept coming into my mind. The smooth little word 'and' makes the transition from theory to practice seem effortless, but I'd rarely found that to be the case. As I recalled thrashing about in the messy gap between the two, I began to see that my novel had stalled because it wasn't the book I needed to write. The book I needed to write concerned breakdowns between theory and practice, and the material was overwhelming. Particles of it had entered my novel and jammed up its works.

An artist once told me that she no longer wanted to make art that looked like art. I was discovering that I no longer wanted to write novels that read like novels. Instead of shapeliness and disguise, I wanted a form that allowed for formlessness and mess. It occurred to me that one way to find that form might be to tell the truth.

As a child I'd often heard, 'Tell the truth and shame the devil'. When the truth was told, someone had to be shamed – usually the teller of truth. It was time, I told myself, to stop fearing shame.

✦

From the age of seven, I sat a piano exam every year. I enjoyed playing the piano, but it was only in the weeks leading up to my exam that I practised every day as prescribed. At its best, my playing was confident and free of mistakes. That was always enough to earn me a Distinction, scraping through with a mark or two to spare.

When I'd been playing for a few years, my teacher entered me for a music theory exam. Each week after my lesson I'd follow her down a corridor to a room where music paper was stacked on a table alongside copies of past exams. My teacher would explain what this or that exercise entailed before returning to the piano room, where her next pupil would already be waiting. Under her guidance, I learned to notate key signatures, pitches, and intervals. I notated scales using accidentals. I transposed short pieces from one key to another. I translated Italian terms into English. On the day of the exam, at a desk in a hall full of children, I carried out all these tasks and others with enjoyment and ease. When my theory result came in, I had an almost perfect score.

The relationship between my theory exercises and the music I played must have been so obvious to my teacher that she neglected to point it out. It wasn't in the least obvious to me. Theory and practice remained distinct activities that occupied separate rooms in my mind. In one I wrote in pencil on paper printed with staves, in the other I struck black and white notes on a keyboard, and no corridor linked the two.

After I received my usual skin-of-the-teeth Distinction for Grade 3 piano, my teacher advised me against attempting Grade 4 the following year. She suggested that I gain time and proficiency by repeating Grade 3 instead.

In 1972 there was no local music board in our freshly postcolonial nation. Two British music boards operated in Sri Lanka, and I'd always taken the exams set by the same one. Perhaps to lessen the sting of the word 'repeat', my teacher now entered me for the other board's exam.

Music exams begin with aural tests administered

by the examiner from the piano. In one test the examiner plays a few bars twice, after which the candidate claps the rhythm of the music. In another test the candidate sings the bars the examiner has played, keeping in key and in time. In a third test the examiner plays a key chord and the tonic, and asks the candidate to sing a specified note further up the scale. Those were the kinds of tests I'd done the previous year. There were others along similar lines, but I've forgotten what they were.

I wore my favourite dress to my second Grade 3 exam: a burnt-orange glazed-cotton shift with a square, pleated yoke and a narrow ruffle at the armholes and neck. When my name was called, I went into the room where my examiner was waiting. Music boards recruit their examiners from teachers, performers, and composers valued for their expertise, and the British boards always sent out examiners from the UK. A thin Englishman was sitting at the piano. He was wearing a tie, but had removed his jacket and rolled up his sleeves.

I clapped the rhythm of the first bars he played, standing, as usual, about a metre to his right. He extended his arm and told me to come closer. I took a step forward, and he repeated the instruction, and so it went until I'd stepped into the circle of his arm.

He was an expert.

The tests continued. I sang and clapped and identified changes in rhythm, and my examiner's right hand stroked my thigh, below my dress at first and then higher.

My examiner's hand slipped into my knickers.

It continued its expert exploration as I played arpeggios and scales sitting on his lap.

A few days later at school, a girl in the class above mine approached me at break. We had the same piano teacher and we'd sat our exams on the same day. I'd turned eleven that year, so she must have been twelve. She asked if our examiner had done 'something funny' to me on Saturday. I told her that he had. We squirmed and giggled and grimaced. We parted. We never spoke of it again.

What were our options?

We were espaliered children, trained in silence, compliance, and respect. We inhabited a world designed for the protection and pleasure of adults. We had no words for abuse and only the haziest notion of sex. What we knew for certain was that everything related to 'down there' was shameful. What we knew for certain was that to attract sexual attention was to be shamed.

We pictured ourselves standing before a parent or a teacher, mumbling that 'something funny had happened down there'.

We pictured ourselves scolded or slapped or beaten as liars with shameless thoughts.

We pictured ourselves scolded or slapped or beaten as girls who wore short, shameless dresses to an exam.

We pictured ourselves ridiculed, the mumbled words that required all our courage mocked. What if 'something funny' turned out to be only an unavoidable step on the way to adulthood? What if it was like menstruation, which we called 'growing up'? What if, like menstruation, it was unmentionable, shameful, and ordinary all at once? What if we were ignorant girls, whose ignorance would double our shame?

Finally, because we were children and therefore still open to miracles, we pictured ourselves believed, held, comforted, even magically avenged. All the while, the shame that issued from our mouths ballooned and ballooned, and the beloved adults who believed, held, comforted, and even magically avenged us were now also trapped forever in the enormous black balloon of shame.

What were our options?

How wise she was, that girl with the pretty, heart-shaped face. She shared her secret so that we could squirm and giggle and pull faces together instead of alone. The way to counter shame was to seek out solidarity. She was only twelve but she understood that.

My results arrived.

Pass With Merit.

No reliable Distinction.

Two complementary explanations: (1) My examiner's

music board had higher standards than the other one, and he'd upheld them; (2) I hadn't played my best that day.

What would happen next? My teacher and I surveyed each other with dismay. Neither of us felt that I was ready for Grade 4, but I could hardly repeat Grade 3 again. The subject was shelved for the little that remained of the year, and what happened next was emigration to Australia. No more piano and no more music lessons, but I found that I didn't really care.

✦

At the start of 1986 I moved from Sydney to Melbourne. I was twenty-four. The first thing I did in Melbourne was buy a vintage dress. The dress was made of lace, and had cap sleeves, an empire waist, and a fitted knee-length skirt. It dated from the early sixties when thousands of its kind must have been made. Now fashion had plucked it from oblivion and filled it with warm young bodies again. Powder-blue and rose and coffee-cream variants existed, but my dress was Intellectual Black. A university in Melbourne had given me money to undertake an MA in English. I turned up on campus to enrol and found two undergrads ahead of me in the queue. 'Be the one to break up,' one of them was urging her friend. 'Be the one. Be the cool one.'

The third important thing I did that week was sign a lease on a flat in St Kilda, a run-down one-bedder at the rear of a Victorian house. Since arriving in Melbourne I'd been staying with Lenny, a friend of Sydney friends. Lenny had a lectureship in art history, and he lived in St Kilda in a flat overlooking the bay. He was a Marxist, like all the young men I knew back then. They were always going on about Late Capitalism, and I admired their optimism. How could they be sure that we weren't stuck in About a Third of the Way Through Capitalism? Or Still Just Revving Up Capitalism? The women I knew described themselves as feminists, and so did I. In theory there was no reason not to be a Marxist feminist, but it was tricky in practice because Marxism in student politics was dominated by men.

While trusting in feminism's transformative power, I retained a stubborn, dazed belief in love. All through my undergraduate years in Sydney I'd valued it as a transcendent ideal. Then I read a letter that I wasn't meant to read. It was addressed to the man I believed loved me, and it was plain that his affair with the letter-writer had been going on for months. She was a smart, good-looking, outspoken feminist in our circle. Her name was Lois – yes, really! Did she call him Superman in bed? That was one of the enraged, feeble, anguished things I howled at the man. Afterwards I went to a park beside the harbour and lay on the grass. I told myself,

Remember this, learn from this. Pineapple-syrup light dripped on everything and sweetened everything except my thoughts. The unpolluted blue overhead was interrupted only by a casuarina's smoky green.

✦

St Kilda was *the* place to live, according to Lenny. 'Always follow the junkies. They've got great judgment in real estate. And they frighten away the gentry, so rents stay low. There are heaps of affordable flats in St Kilda, and you've got the beach as well.'

The beach was ordinary after Sydney, but St Kilda wasn't an ordinary place. Having come down in the world, it made room for the delusional, the down-and-out, the sad. Late Capitalism preferred to shroud its facts in velvet, but here they showed brutal and plain. People sat blank-eyed in parks, walked the streets raging or muttering, queued at the Sacred Heart Mission for a meal. A woman shuffled along in nightie and dressing gown, calling to Frankie – a passer-by said she'd been calling for years. The shimmer of disaster was always close at hand. Someone would scream abuse, a chair would hurtle through a window. Junkies shot up in laneways and sometimes died there; dawn's calling card was a siren. After nightfall, Grey Street and its tributaries lit up with sparkly eyeshadow and expanses of pearly flesh:

people selling their only asset had to be visible in the dark.

Violent, and violently policed, St Kilda should have been depressing. But it lay open to sea and sky, and a sense of possibility flowed from that. When the estate agent handed me my keys, I headed away from my flat, towards the pier. Others, too, were walking out to sea in the carbolic summer light. We gathered at the end of the pier, where the breakwater began. My companions were weathered old men in shorts, copper statues with gnarly knees. We contemplated the water and the floating gulls, the distant music of trams at our backs. That salty blue water was full of life I couldn't name. I'd spent the past two years working for a market research company, where every nugget of information that could be extracted from a consumer at the other end of a phone was sorted, classified, and assigned a numerical code. Knowledge was different: unbounded, endlessly renewed. I wanted the roll and slosh of its depths beneath me, the risk of drowning. I wanted it to carry me beyond the limits of myself.

✦

In a secondhand anthology of North American poetry, I came across a postcard of the Cirque d'Hiver building in Paris. It was marking the place of a poem by Elizabeth Bishop called 'Cirque d'Hiver'. I Blu

Tacked the postcard to the peeling wall above my desk, typed out the poem and put that up, too. I added my poster of Virginia Woolf, and a quote from Gramsci: 'The crisis consists precisely in the fact that the old is dying and the new cannot be born; in this interregnum a great variety of morbid symptoms appear.' I was a feminist, and my morbid symptom was wanting Lois dead. Of course I blamed my ex, too, for our break-up, but not to the same ferocious, wounded extent. Who, among everyone on the planet, can we never forgive for a failure of protection? MOTHER. Everything follows from there. Feminism was delivering body blows to the patriarchy, but the new world of steadfast female solidarity was still struggling to be born.

◆

Lenny always looked angry and was unfailingly kind. He was red of face, serious-minded, and possessed many friends. His friends furnished my flat, a wingback yellow armchair here, a futon there, everything given, lent, or sold for a few bucks. The futon-giver threw in a disquisition on futons. Weighty Australian futons were nothing like the original Japanese ones, which were essentially thin quilts, 'like medieval mattresses', piled on top of one other for sleeping and hung from windows to air. He couldn't give me a slatted bedframe, so advised turning the futon over now and then to avert 'a mould situation' – advice I forgot at once.

There was a fireplace in my lounge room, minus a mantelpiece but with a veined, reddish marble surround. A board was nailed across the bottom of the chimney. The nails were rusty, which meant that no fire had been lit in the hearth for years, but a smell of cold ashes persisted. It had once been a spacious room, quite possibly beautiful, but flimsy walls had carved it into three. A sliver of hallway and bathroom along one side were answered by a slice of bedroom and kitchen on the other.

My books arrived from Sydney. They filled my donated bookcase and spread to the carpet's vomity orange swirls. Lenny came to dinner. He inspected my books, held up *Homage to Catalonia*, and said that when Franco died, Barcelona ran out of champagne. He read 'Cirque d'Hiver' aloud to himself, under his breath. The mechanical horse the poem described was not unlike him, glossy of eye and smart.

Lenny had brought me wine in a small, fancy cask and the news that he'd just bought an Apple Mac. He was going to throw a party for the Mac, he said. Even the look of the invitation he handed me announced that it came from a different world. The party details were set out in a mix of sans-serif fonts contained in grey-stippled geometric shapes. When I saw it I got the impression that something profound had collapsed.

Whatever was coming would be difficult and thrilling, and the Mac was bound up in it. I looked at my typewriter – my dear typewriter! my dependable blue Smith Corona! – and saw it turn into a ghost.

Pale lines flashed on Lenny's wrist as he forked up dhal. He'd alluded to them once, saying that he couldn't recommend growing up gay in a country town. Now he wondered aloud what Australia had been like for me. 'We're such racist shits.'

Another thing Lenny told me was that for a long time the artist he'd admired most was Caravaggio. 'I can't look at those paintings these days. Everyone in them looks ill.'

◆

'I was very relieved and happy to hear that you have found a nice flat and made some nice friends. Lenny must be earning very well if he is a Lecturer. Is he saving for a house or is his flat an own-your-own? Do you see him a lot? How nice that he likes Sri Lankan food. I'm enclosing a recipe for gotu kola mallung. It can be made with cabbage leaves instead. According to Babs, St Kilda is not a good suburb and only prostitutes live there. I told her that Lenny is a Lecturer so that can't be true! Please take care and do not go out alone after dark. Do not open your door without knowing who is there.'

✦

A boxy object in orthopaedic non-colour stood on Lenny's desk, where a bunch of gay guys had gathered. I joined them in time to hear Lenny, seated at the desk, explain that personal computers were an opportunity to seize the means of communication. He amazed us by demonstrating a few things the Apple Mac could do.

In the kitchen I found a bowl, a board, and a knife, and began cutting up the mangoes I'd brought. That was when I met Olivia and Amabel, who came in looking for paper cups. They were big, fair, marble-fleshed women who brought confidence to the way they occupied space. Amabel had the centre-parted hair and discontented mouth of a Botticelli Madonna. She was even taller than tall Olivia, and her round white face was a clock. The clock took its time inspecting my dress, my Docs and my offering of mangoes. It smiled as if alarmed.

I chatted to Shaz, who played sax in a feminist band called Says Ann. Twisting her platinum ponytail, she said she was trying to decide if she should give in and join the public service, or stay on the dole and hope that the band got a big break. Whenever people talked about office work, I remembered my fellow commuters in Sydney rising on escalators in the morning, all of us looking professional and stunned.

The party was for Shaz as well as for the Mac. A property developer had bought the block of flats where she lived and issued all the tenants with eviction notices. Lenny had drawn up a petition on the Mac and printed it out. It was addressed to the St Kilda council and our local MP, and called for action against the developers who were moving into the suburb, doing up flats and driving out renters. I took it out to the people drinking on the balcony. Amabel was there, telling someone called Kit that she found toenail polish 'cheap'. She stared at my Docs, as if she could see through them to my feet.

The balcony people signed the petition, and I hung around there for a while. Kit had one of those faces with bones that look hard. He paid no attention to me, which was a pity. He rested his stubbie on the wall and turned away to the view. I learned that Olivia was Amabel's cousin, and that they shared a house in Fitzroy. Olivia was in her fourth year of music-law, and Amabel was in her second year of law-law. Amabel's father, a professor of something, was called Pobby, and her mother, a gallerist, was called Mops.

Olivia joined us on the balcony. She wore her yellow hair in plaits woven around her head like a fairy-tale girl. Her smile passed from left to right, pausing halfway as if stuck. Kit placed his chin on top of her head and his arms around her, and Olivia leaned back against his chest.

Back inside, a friend of Lenny's described the Mac as 'a technology of enchantment'. Benedict had an earring and worked in a bookshop; we'd met when I was staying in Lenny's flat. He was a Kiwi, but had the sunless, underfed look of an English punk. Cops liked to stop him in the street and order him to roll up his sleeves so they could check his arms for track marks. He told me about the helpline where Lenny and he volunteered. 'It's mostly married men calling. Everyone's scared. I mean, *really* scared.'

Amabel materialised at my elbow. 'Lenny says you speak French. What's French for greenhouse gas? It's on the tip of my tongue.'

The whole room seemed to fall silent, as if everyone was listening for my reply. I said, 'I've been working for the past two years. I haven't kept up my French.'

'I'll remember in a minute,' said Amabel, 'and then I'll tell you how to say it.'

Kit and Olivia had joined a knot of people that included Shaz. Kit was telling her that the flat below his would become vacant soon. His building had a rooftop garden with great views, and his flat on the top floor was incredibly good value. He shared a bathroom with his neighbour but he didn't mind: 'It's bohemian.' I wondered who got to clean the bohemian bathroom but I didn't have the nerve to ask.

Shaz said that there was always Lenny's couch if she hadn't found somewhere to live by the end of the month. She wouldn't mind moving, she went on. Her flat was a dump and also a bit creepy. Sometimes she'd go home and find that small changes had occurred in her absence. A cupboard she was sure she'd closed would be open, or a cushion from the lounge would be lying on her bed. It was like being in a confusing dream. 'You know – where things are different from the way they should be.'

Someone said the obvious thing: 'Junkies.'

'I'm on the top floor. I've never missed cash and, apart from my saxophone, I've got nothing a junkie could flog. And it happens regularly, like a few times a month. There are mornings I wake up and something's changed overnight. I'd have moved out ages ago, but the rent's really low.'

Olivia said that a ghost visited her from time to time. Pieces of jewellery kept vanishing from her room. 'Nothing valuable, nothing worth stealing. But special things. Like a bead bracelet that I used to wear a lot, and one of my favourite earrings.'

'You've got a poltergeist,' said Benedict. 'Same as Shaz.'

'The poltergeist is my mother. When she died she left me her jewellery, but I never wear it. So she's punishing me by taking away the things I like best.' Olivia touched the small golden heart that hung at her neck. 'Kit gave me this. I never take it off, never, I *sleep* in it to keep it safe.'

She looked at Kit with an expression that made me embarrassed for her, or maybe envious, I couldn't say.

✦

The English department at my university in Sydney had a Designated Feminist, and Melbourne had one, too. Melbourne's Designated Feminist was called Paula, and she'd agreed to supervise my thesis, 'The Construction of Gender in the Late Fiction of Virginia Woolf'. At our first meeting Paula asked for a chapter outline and gave me a list of secondary reading. 'It's basic,' she said, 'but we find it helps bring Sydney graduates up to speed.'

I embarked on Paula's list and made a discovery. In the time I'd spent away from study, French post-structuralist theory – Theory – had conquered the humanities. When I said so to Lenny, he informed me that Melbourne had been 'Theorised for years'. He was astounded to hear that I'd read some Barthes and Genette, but no Derrida or Foucault. 'But I thought you did combined honours in English and French.'

'Everything French was an affront to the English department,' I explained. 'And the French department's Contemporary Theory unit was taught by a guy who specialised in Sade. At the start of my honours year, he was identified as the campus rapist and arrested. I'm pretty sure the unit's still on hold.'

'Sydney is so backward,' Lenny said with Melbourne glee.

✦

Like Lenny's Mac, Theory announced that the future was now. To mark its arrival, Theory had taken book, essay, novel, story, poem, and play, and replaced them all with text. Theory rejected binaries, exposed aporias, and posited. It posited that meaning was unstable and endlessly deferred. I was good at languages and relished the prospect of learning a new one. Theory took words I knew and used them in startling new ways. I worked out what it meant by *jouissance*, familiar to me only in a non-textual context. I discovered that 'foreground' had become a verb. I practised using '*différance*' and 'logocentric' and 'will-to-power' in sentences. I noted all my findings on index cards. I valued the cards as signifiers of serious scholarship, and boosted my spirits with several packs.

Theory's take on feminism departed from the feminist theory I'd read. Theory was focused on the Symbolic Order and viewed the overthrowing of the patriarchy as an outmoded aim. One could not overthrow the Father, who was *always already* dead, although his phallus was everywhere in society and culture. French feminist thinkers posited that revolution resided in the

Maternal, which was archaic, pre-verbal, pre-Oedipal, linked to rhythms and colours and tones. I sensed that beautiful, radical ideas swam in their contentions, but they eluded my attempts to haul them into view.

After a day spent with Theory, I'd come away from the library feeling headachey and crushed. My undergraduate years had taken on the aspect of a wasteland. The foundations on which I'd expected to build were mere rubble underfoot. To understand Theory, I had to master Continental philosophy going back to the Greeks. I had to read Derrida, Irigaray, Kristeva, Cixous, Foucault, Lacan, Nietzsche, Deleuze, *and* Guattari. I spent evenings lying on my bed, rereading Woolf's novels, all the while feeling guilty that I wasn't reading Theory. Everything important that happened in that flat happened in my bed.

✦

Antigone – Anti to all – rented a flat in the same small deco building as Lenny. She was a goddess warrior who looked like Patti Smith but with much stormier hair. Anti taught part-time in a high school and spent the rest of the week making art. Fabulous, womblike sculptures created from wire, string, and baker's plaster threw complicated shadows on her walls. We liked to drink gin on her balcony, watching the sun crash sullenly into the bay. The bay was a mocking reminder of my thirst for knowledge as Anti asked how my thesis was going. I talked about Theory. I talked about Paula. 'Her lipstick is this really complex red, and I lust after it, but the thing is half of it's on her teeth.'

'You cannot respect a woman with lipstick teeth,' said Anti. 'It's like the principal at my school. She wears tights with brogues. If you insist on wearing brogues you obviously need to flash some bare leg. Otherwise you look like you belong in the royal family.'

We dissected a few more style crimes, but I was soon back on Theory. Theory had identified an authentically female way of writing, I told Anti. The Maternal sentence was liquid and nonlinear, swooping and looping, multidirectional, whorled. It disrupted norms. French feminists revered Woolf as a prime example of a writer in whose work the disruptive Maternal could be observed.

'So that's all great, sort of,' I said. 'What's bothering me is the idea that there's only one authentic way for women to write. It seems very Frenchly authoritarian. You know – like French fashion tells us there's only one correct female silhouette this season, and we all have to be billowing or curvy or streamlined until we're ordered to change. A lot of Woolf's most subversive thinking about women comes in pretty straightforward prose.'

Anti was of the view that we had the right to lift-and-separate sentences as well as burned-my-bra sentences. She said that what the Maternal meant to her was smock dresses. 'Remember them? I made myself one. Cotton velvet, electric blue with loose-petalled orange flowers. I loved myself sick in that dress. Winter 1975. I was sixteen. This bitch, our neighbour, asked my mum if I'd gone and got pregnant.'

What her story showed, I said, was that female experience was inseparable from everyday reality. French feminism conceived of the Maternal as an abstraction, but what the maternal brought women was loss of income and pooey nappies. 'Our lives always come down to money and shit.'

That got us onto women's dependence on men. Anti wasn't against it if it was entered into with 'lucidity and purpose'. Self-sufficiency was a feminist fantasy, she went on. We all depended on other people – that was the meaning of society. 'And who's got all the power in our society? Old Anglo men. Look at us – first-generation migrants. Can our parents push us up the ladder like Anglo parents push their kids? No. Especially not if we have' – inserting her ringed hands into her hair and raising it even higher – 'exquisite, *big* dreams. That's where someone like Ed enters the equation. He's forty-eight, and he's been swimming in the art world from before I was born. Ed can get me a better gallery, get critics to my shows. He takes me fancy places, introduces me to fancy people. Like this woman who's offered me cheap, huge studio space. Also I like fucking Ed.'

She poured us a third gin. 'Are you doing any fucking, baby? I think some really great *jouissance* is what you need.'

✦

The phone rang. Amabel said, 'It's *gaz à effet de serre*.'

✦

Paula set up a meeting to discuss my progress, but I cancelled it at the last minute. In the library that afternoon, I was heading for the stairs when her voice floated up. I ducked into the toilets. Safe in my cubicle, I heard her come in saying, '. . . recurring dream in which I axe-murder Myron.'

Myron had the named chair in English. 'Oh, I have that dream, too,' said Paula's friend. 'Except I shoot him. I keep shooting, and he's on the floor full of bullet holes but he still keeps talking. On and *on*.'

✦

A film called *My Life Without Steve* was previewing in St Kilda. Gillian Leahy, an Australian filmmaker, had written and directed it, and I'd never seen anything like her film. It covered a year in the life of Liz, whose boyfriend had left her for another woman. Shot from Liz's point of view, the film was set entirely within her flat. One window looked out at a slice of Sydney Harbour, but the film was about interiority. Liz was angry, obsessive, depressed. She ruminated on the break-up in a voiceover, trying to work out where things had gone wrong. She read letters and old diary entries aloud. She brooded over photos of happier times. She turned to books for understanding and advice. She quoted Colette and Barthes. She argued with her mother. She sang Dylan and Patsy Cline, songs about the aching end of love. She raged.

I thought, I didn't know that this could be art. It was the first time I'd seen my everyday, unglamorous world in a film. It made me tremble a little. Liz and I owned the same paperbacks, books with a Virago apple or a Women's Press iron on the spine. We had the same aluminium teapot with a turquoise lid, the same cream telephone handset, the same open pantry shelves. Liz's bed linen and curtains were blue, so I guessed that we shared a favourite colour. But these were only superficial, if spooky, correspondences. What made my heart run like a hare was hearing my mind exposed. Liz raged against Steve but equally against his new lover, Jenny. Jenny was a feminist, and so were Liz and her friends. Her friends disapproved of Liz's jealousy and fury. I'd encountered that disapproval, too – or, rather, I'd anticipated it. Sneakier than Liz, I'd raged silently, inwardly, censored by an internal critic who found jealousy a trite, despicable emotion, a morbid symptom that ran counter to feminist practice. Once or twice, I'd run into Lois by chance. Envisioning her disembowelled, I'd smiled sweetly and got away fast.

One day I summoned the courage or the despair to tell a friend that I'd been betrayed. She laughed. I sounded like a character in a nineteenth-century novel, she said. She was wrong: I was thoroughly up to date. Gillian Leahy understood. She'd made a film about the interregnum and its messy human truths. Jenny/Lois was a morbid symptom and so was Liz/I.

At the end of the film, as I was crossing the foyer, I heard my name. Kit came up to me. We moved to one side and, standing near a wall, inspected each other. He had blue-grey eyes, northern eyes in the south. Their colour intensified his aura of bony lightness. People carried on streaming past us, putting on their jackets. Kit asked what I'd thought of the film.

'I loved it. It captured what that woman felt so brilliantly.'

He was silent.

'What about you?'

He ran his hand through his bright brown hair. 'I found it a bit . . . exaggerated? There were those guys working on those boats outside her place. She could have just gone down and invited one of them up.'

Men were marvellous, truly. Had a single woman in the audience noticed the guys on the boats? They were insignificant figures, literally tiny, barely in the picture. In offering us an intimate experience of female suffering, the film had asked us to pay attention to Liz. Kit's remark was a kind of violence, a knife thrust into a painting. I was repelled by it, and at the same time it struck me as a form of truth. Theory taught us to do what Kit had done: to notice what was unimportant, to read against the grain, to take apart what was presented as immutable and put it together in a different way.

But.

I said that what he expected Liz to do wasn't a simple thing.

'Isn't it?'

I thought about that.

The world tipped, poured, glittered.

My flat wasn't far away, but it seemed as if we'd never arrive. While we were in the cinema, the wind had swung around. I hadn't brought a jacket, and my broderie anglaise top had flower-shaped cut-outs in the cloth. By the time we got to my place, little flowers of cold were printed along my arms and across my chest.

✦

We were talking in bed one evening, with a lamp shining and the radio softly on, when the phone rang. I knew it was my mother because she liked to call when the interstate rate was cheaper. Incapable of letting a call from her go unanswered, I told her that I was studying and would ring back the next day. After that, whenever Kit called me or buzzed my intercom, he'd ask if I felt like studying.

We never made arrangements in advance but said, 'See you soon,' on parting. Kit always came around on Monday and Thursday, and sometimes on Sunday or Tuesday as well. I never saw him on Friday or Saturday or Wednesday, and I assumed that he was with Olivia on those days. I don't remember discussing it, but I never went to his place – I suppose because Olivia could have turned up there or called. If I thought of her, it was with triumph and something like scorn. I believed that I deserved Kit more, although if I'd been asked why, I couldn't have explained.

✦

Lenny and I were having lunch at the Galleon. Our favourite waitress, a Dane who smelled of minty toothpaste, had seated us at the table we liked for its sparkly red Formica top. Lenny mentioned that Kit's parents were visiting Melbourne and that he was looking forward to seeing them that evening. I asked where they were going for dinner, and he said that Olivia was having everyone around.

I knew that Kit's father was a pharmacist, and that Lenny's mother had worked for him for years. It was only to be expected that Kit's parents would want to see Lenny, but I felt sad that I was excluded from meeting them. Something shifted after that. I couldn't stop picturing everyone sitting around a table that Olivia had set with a tablecloth, heavy cutlery, and ironed serviettes. Kit's parents would praise the food she put before them, and later, taking off their watches and shoes in their hotel room, they'd tell each other yet again how fortunate it was that Kit had ended up with such a lovely girl. Kit would have his degree in mining engineering by the end of the year, Olivia would graduate a year later, and then the wedding could take place.

All weekend the film played in my mind. Kit's mother was tall and handsome like her son, with the same smooth skin that tanned. His father, a talented tennis player in his youth, had a paunch now, and a velvety birthmark on his neck.

✦

Lying on his back as his semen dried on my breasts, Kit said, 'I feel so hemmed in by my family sometimes.' I waited for him to say more, but he only reached for a tissue. I got up and made coffee, heating the milk first. Kit had told me that, inspired by my example, he'd started warming the milk for his coffee, and I wondered if Olivia now did the same.

When I returned to the bedroom, he'd found my copy of Barthes' *A Lover's Discourse* and was reading it, propped up against pillows. I thought, That's how he'll look when he's married to Olivia, sitting at the breakfast table with their children, reading the *Age*. I told him that my favourite line in the book was 'Who will write the history of tears?' Kit said he could have guessed that – I'd underlined it twice. I reminded him that Liz had quoted from *A Lover's Discourse* in *My Life Without Steve*. Kit asked if he could borrow the book. I showed him my name on the flyleaf and waited for him to realise that he'd have to risk Olivia seeing it. He said, 'Maybe not.'

◆

In 1986 critics applying Theory to literary texts liked to cast themselves as torturers. The text told a story, but that story was a screen. The critic was obliged to 'probe' and 'interrogate' the text in order to make it 'yield' the story it was concealing. The critic *always already* knew every detail of that story, but it was necessary to make the text confess. Applying pressure to soft, secret places, the critic exposed fake oppositions, crude essentialisms, bourgeois hegemonies, totalising mechanisms, humanist teleologies, squalid repressions, influential aporias, and many more textual fragilities. The text bucked and shrieked under the critic's ministrations, but the critic was merciless. Things always ended the same way: the text came apart, divulging its hidden significance. That was The Story Under The Story. When it was revealed and the text was in pieces, the critic had won.

✦

'I've made a note not to ring you on Mondays or Thursdays because you attend seminars on those evenings. Make sure you are eating well and staying strong. You sound very busy, which I can well understand. It poured all last night and all day today. Let me know if there is <u>anything</u> you want from here, even money.'

✦

Kit came from a town planted with grand, spreading trees renowned for their autumn colour. Winters there often brought snow. Snow always falls sideways, Kit told me, never straight down. Another thing he said was that autumn pigments are present year-round in leaves. In spring and summer, they're overpowered by chlorophyll. Cold weather fades the green, and the golds and reds are revealed.

What I knew about him would have covered only a medium-size index card. I knew that his mother's people owned a horse stud, because he'd joked that the family fortune came from semen. I knew that he had a younger sister still at school and an older one who was temping in London – their names were Alice and Meg. I knew that he'd had a pony and played the trumpet as a child. I knew that he owned an expensive camera and had done a course in photography – he'd love to make it his career, he said, but that was only a dream. He often talked in his sleep, soft, veiled speeches that caused him to tug at the bedding. One blue-black dawn, as rain slid down, I watched him turn on his side and murmur while smiling. His world, too, remained stubbornly obscure to me, a Russian expanse of shadowy steppes.

◆

I told Lenny that I was struggling with Paula's reading list. We were walking out along the pier late one evening when I confessed. The fidgety darkness ahead of us eased the shame of the confession, and so did not having to look Lenny in the face. 'Paula's so . . . black leather jacket,' said Lenny, whose wardrobe consisted of shapeless jeans and flannelette shirts. 'We had to recruit someone to sit on this faculty committee, right, and a name comes up, an older woman, a linguist who's done admirable work with Aboriginal communities, and Paula says, "But she's a liberal humanist!" So we end up with this bloke instead, he's got a black leather jacket, too, and he calls himself a Foucauldian and a feminist, and any pretty undergrad can tell you what a sleazy prick he is. But we've been spared a liberal humanist, hoo-bloody-ray.'

'Liberal humanists are the *worst*, Lenny. They're the forces of reaction and must be destroyed. Even I know that.'

'Artists used to think about art through art. Now they think about it through Theory. What happened to praxis? The left used to dream of doing. You know what I see all the time in tutorials? Women, working-class kids, kids from migrant backgrounds, the kinds of students who used to feel empowered by feminism and Marxism, struggling to engage with the Theory they're expected to read now.'

Leaning on the guardrail at the end of the pier, Lenny told me to forget Paula's list. 'Just read a couple of those guides to Theory like that one by Eagleton. Or Culler's *On Deconstruction*. It's what the postgrads in my department do.'

It was excellent, practical advice. I filled another pack of index cards with notes. Then I read only revelatory essays about fiction by brilliant female scholars armoured in feminism but not mesmerised by Theory. Paula was one of them. I've never forgotten her unweaving of *The Rainbow*. It genuflected at Theory, but that was only a ritual to sanctify the essay's serious, chewy business, namely the mauling of D. H. Lawrence. Paula had chestnut ringlets like a character from Jane Austen and big blue ponds for eyes. Nature had designed these things to deflect male attention from her bloody teeth. She feasted on raw patriarchal stupidity, and when I exchanged the library for the chilly dark of an autumn evening, my mind was hosting fireworks. At the end of the brick walkway I liked to look back at the library, at its glowing calm. I planned to spend the term researching, and to start writing after the May break. I was lapped by happiness in those weeks, stroking time as it passed.

✦

My mother took a long time to answer when I rang. She'd come home with a headache, she said. She processed claims for Medicare, and seldom saw anyone outside of work, although she talked to her sister on the phone. My aunt had a house, two sons, and a white husband who, although alcoholic, was alive, so my mother didn't enjoy their conversations. When I asked what she was planning to do on the weekend, she said that she had a couple of nice books.

In my first undergraduate year at uni, a professor whose dog I walked invited me to her sixtieth birthday party. It was held in Glebe on a mild-mannered evening at the end of spring. The professor's tall house was full of light. Her sister was playing the cello in one of her splendid rooms. There were speeches on the terrace, and champagne. A long table covered in a damask cloth offered ham, pink roast beef, smoked salmon, quiches, salads, dark, chewy bread, a giant bowl of strawberries, a wheel of French cheese.

The party took place in what turned out to be the last week of my father's life. His appetite was undiminished, but he found swallowing painful and was existing on liquids, taken in sips. My mother was starving herself because the smell of cooking was a torture to him. I'd prepare meals for her and take them around and later discover them untouched in the fridge. When I confronted my mother, she said that my father could smell food heating in the microwave – I don't know what she was living on, ice cream maybe. In Glebe I stood against a wall with a heaped plate, and the dog's hopeful, upward gaze at my knee. The evening was unfolding slowly, as if time were an invalid dragging its feet. Everything I looked at had the false vividness of a film. I smiled at people in beautiful, understated clothes and listened to them discuss their holiday plans. Seven kilometres to the west, my father lay dying in a rented flat.

When I'd eaten everything on my plate I went back for seconds. Before leaving, I ignored the powder room off the hallway and ran lightly upstairs. In a bathroom there I scooped hand cream from a jar and flushed it away. Then I crammed perfume, makeup, and a thickly soft face washer into my bag. At the last minute I added a cake of jasmine-scented soap. I wanted to join the bourgeoisie and I wanted to destroy it. As soon as I made it back to my share house, I threw up.

✦

From time to time I offered Kit a magisterial lie that came spinning out of my brain like silk. The sole purpose of these myths was to cloak me in glamour and mystique. There was the night I claimed to have been in a relationship with Iva Davies when Icehouse was still called Flowers. In fact, I went on, I was the one who came up with the band's new name, inspired by my freezing student house. In fact, I'd never taken the slightest interest in Flowers/Icehouse/Davies, but that morning, waiting at the tram stop, I'd heard 'Great Southern Land' drift from a passing car.

✦

Since the death of my father, responsibility for my mother had devolved upon me. Now she was my child as well as my mother. My daughter-mother loved eye-shrivelling colours, and ezi-care fabrics held together by sheen. She buried her perfect, poreless complexion under makeup as slabby as concrete. As well as dyeing her hair in an obvious way, she did something to it that made it look as if it would be unpleasant to touch. For her part, she feared that my secondhand clothing harboured disease. My nesty armpits repelled her, as did my mismatched earrings and my Docs. We cringed at and were embarrassed by each other's self-presentation. Why were our daughters inviting censure and shame by breaking the rules?

✦

I was supplementing my scholarship with a few hours of teaching language-lab classes for the French department. As I left the lab one morning, I ran into Olivia. 'Hi,' she said, putting so much wide-eyed surprise into it that I decided she'd been waiting for me. She asked if I'd like to have coffee one day. I suggested meeting in St Kilda – the coffee would be better than anything we could find on campus – and she agreed.

My usual hangout was the Galleon, but I arranged to meet Olivia at Leo's. It was a subtle insult. Leo's was a showplace, patronised by the respectable who came to St Kilda to gawp. On that Friday afternoon I arrived early and sat facing the window. A chill wind was blowing along Fitzroy Street, where plane trees were dropping their leather-veined leaves. I felt sure that Olivia was going to confront me about Kit, and I was still debating whether to feign outrage or say 'So what?' That morning I'd come close to calling her to cancel, pleading a cold.

Trams clattered past, under the jostling clouds. I watched Olivia cross the street. She was wearing the kind of thing she wore, a windcheater and jeans. Her hair had been scraped off her face and hung down her back in a long plait. There was a stillness in the way she held herself that I'd noticed in Amabel, too – it was the composure of their kind.

Olivia placed her bag on a spare chair, and I complimented her on its buttery brown leather. Then I said that I'd expected her to be carrying a bigger bag. She looked puzzled. 'Clothes for the weekend,' I explained. As I spoke, I realised that she probably left spare clothing at Kit's.

'Oh, I'm not going to Kit's tonight. He usually comes to my place on Fridays but he's got a huge assignment due next week.'

She asked if I had plans for the weekend. I chatted to her brightly: about my thesis, about Shaz, now in a share house in East St Kilda, about Simone de Beauvoir, who'd died that week. We discovered that we'd both devoured de Beauvoir's autobiography. Olivia said, 'The life she created with Sartre, the way they refused to do what society and their families expected of them. I admire that so much.' She'd written to de

Beauvoir just months before to thank her for her work. 'I'm so glad I did that now.'

My coffee and Olivia's tea came. She'd asked for her tea bag on the side, and she dunked it briefly in her cup before taking it out and adding milk. She offered me the sugar, and I declined. She added two spoonfuls to her tea, saying, 'That's why you're so slim.' I used to take three sugars, I told her, but my share house ran out one evening after the shops had closed, and from that day I did without. To be honest, I'd never taken more than two sugars, but I exaggerated to make her feel better. 'Chuck out your sugar when the shops are shut,' I urged her. 'See how you go.'

Olivia's blunt hands looked strong as she stirred her tea, but when she took her spoon from her cup, it slipped from her grasp. I guessed that her palms were sweaty. She shot me a sheepish smile and wiped her hands on a serviette from the dispenser. She folded and refolded the serviette into a strip, folded that in half, and slid it under her saucer.

She told me she'd been born in Western Australia. Her mother was a teacher and her father was a geologist. They split up when Olivia was nine, and she moved east with her mother. Pobby and Mops, Olivia's uncle and aunt, had a large property at Mount Macedon, and the two families had formed a household there. I wasn't about to expose my parents to Olivia's scrutiny, so when she asked about my family, I gave little away and countered with more questions of my own. We discovered that her mother and my father had died within months of each other. Olivia's father had remarried and still lived in Perth – she spoke of him in an indifferent, queenly way.

She took off her windcheater, revealing an open-neck red shirt printed with sprigs of white flowers. It was good to see that she'd kept her necklace safe, I told her. At once her hand flew to the small golden heart. Another piece of jewellery had vanished just that week, she said. While she was telling me about it, I was thinking about Kit's long brown back in my shower. He would grope for a facecloth and dab soap from his eyes like a child.

Olivia broke off her story, and her face went blotchy. She was gazing over my shoulder, so I looked around. A woman with fair, faded hair had risen from a table and was taking leave of her friends, putting on her jacket.

When I turned back, Olivia's skin was still mottled. I asked if everything was all right, and she looked as if she didn't understand. Then she said, 'That lady in the navy jacket. For a minute I thought she was my mother.' It was a silly mistake, she continued, it had happened before. After her mother died, Olivia had cleared out her wardrobe and taken boxes of clothes to a recycle shop. Since then, she'd twice mistaken someone for her mother because the stranger was wearing what seemed to be her mother's clothes. 'That jacket could easily have been hers. She liked tailored clothing. She used to have a blue jacket like that.'

Throughout our conversation, Olivia was unable to look at me for very long and kept glancing away. I knew what she wanted to ask and that she was afraid of both the asking and the answer, and also that she knew I could see her fear. I felt an overwhelming pity for her then, in a powerless way, as if observing an animal whose suffering I'd neither brought about nor could end. I'd often told myself that the situation wasn't fair to Olivia. But immediately I'd think, It's nothing to do with me, the problem's between her and Kit. I was making the same discovery that Lois had made: in the circumstances, what mattered was to be fair to myself.

After we parted, I was haunted by the impression that I'd talked too much, said stupid things and lied through my teeth. Why must you jangle? I asked myself, in the Condiments aisle at the supermarket. When I got home, there was a photograph in my letterbox. The image had a childlike simplicity and power: a grassy hill on whose gentle crest a few sheep were grazing, unevenly spaced. The message on the back said, 'Feel like studying tonight?' Violent, triumphant joy seized me, a volt at first, then a warmth that spread in my chest.

✦

My mind kept returning to Leo's, and I'd be sitting opposite Olivia, watching her stir her tea. I wondered if Kit knew that we'd seen each other. I didn't tell him, because mentioning her felt awkward. Late one Sunday he arrived at my flat, smelling of mud and cold air. He'd come straight to me from a weekend spent with his folk in the country, he said. 'All I could think about, the whole weekend, was studying with you.'

Watching him get dressed the next morning, I silently practised, Does Olivia know about us? Finally I said it. It came out overloud.

Kit went on tying his shoelace. 'We have a deconstructed relationship,' he said.

The calculated way he said 'deconstructed' amused me – he was producing the price of admission to the palace of cool. I remembered him saying 'bohemian' with the same self-conscious air. Once he'd breezily claimed that he'd had the marks to get into medicine at Melbourne Uni but 'it didn't appeal'. He hadn't explained why he wound up doing engineering at RMIT, but he was prickly about it. The Arts crowd he hung out with looked on engineering students as the antithesis of cool. As for RMIT, it wasn't Melbourne Uni and that was that.

'Does that mean Olivia has another lover, too?' I asked, suppressing a smile.

'There's no need to bring her into this.' Moments passed. He said, 'I love her.' He sounded angry and startled, as if unwelcome news had caught him off guard.

His declaration infuriated me. Olivia was welcome to his deconstructed love! I was a modern woman, perfectly content with his body's undeconstructed need of mine. Each time we met confirmed that need. He said, 'When we're studying, the pieces of my life slot into place.' He said that seeing me on Lenny's balcony, the first time we'd met, he'd had to turn away to hide his erection. 'I wanted to grab your arm and tell you, "What do these people matter? Why are we still here?"'

✦

We didn't have meals – proper meals – together. If we felt hungry, we ate Vegemite toast. Sometimes Kit had an apple. Apples were his favourite fruit, so although I didn't like them, I'd started buying a couple for him each week.

He turned up early one evening with a big foil-covered dish. He'd made lasagne. 'My speciality. Lenny's mum's, actually. She showed us both how, and we had to take turns cooking it until we got it right.'

The lasagne went into the oven, and we ate it with what formality we could muster. I'd put jars in the fireplace and set a lighted candle in each one, and we had squares of kitchen towel for serviettes. At one point, as we talked, Kit mentioned that his bike had skidded on tram tracks, and he'd been lucky not to come off. I said that I'd always wanted to ride a bike. When I was small, our neighbour had a bike accident that left him with a permanent limp, so my mother hadn't let me learn. 'Who is *always* to blame?' I ended dramatically, and answered myself: 'Mother!'

Kit offered to teach me to ride. He said, 'I'll bring my bike, and we'll go up to the park.' The strangeness of that picture, the two of us side by side in the open, bright world, strolling through autumn, struck us at the same moment. Softened by wine, we began to laugh. Our hours together were inseparable from lamplight, from crusts on a plate beside my futon, from the dusty smell of the blow heater. I put the leftover lasagne in the fridge and the dish to soak in the sink. On the radio, a woman sang, 'You and me, you and me, you and me, you and me, baby . . .'

In the morning I tried to return Kit's dish, but he insisted on giving it to me. He said he only made lasagne when he was procrastinating, which he couldn't afford to do. 'It's a nice dish, isn't it,' he went on. 'It goes with your plates.' The plates were willow-patterned china from the Sacred Heart charity shop, and I was touched that he'd noticed them. It was indeed a nice dish, white enamel with a dark blue rim.

✦

The rumours that had been circulating of a major nuclear accident in the Soviet Union were confirmed that day. I was about to run out of clean knickers, so I went to the laundromat. The phone was ringing when I got back. My mother wanted to know if Australia was safe from the fallout. 'Of course,' I said, thinking, Who knows? She asked if Sydney was more at risk than Melbourne, given that it was further north. What she was telling me was that I'd abandoned her to nuclear contamination when I moved south. I passed on advice I'd heard on the radio: stick with root vegetables for a while and avoid leafy greens. Obviously she would carry on eating as she pleased, because who is the woman who does as her mother advises? We'd rather be independent and dead.

I realised how absurd it would be for Kit and me to die alone when all that separated us was a few suburban blocks. For the first time I dialled his number. Almost at once, I regretted my impulse. As I was hanging up, I thought he answered. But the connection was broken, and it felt silly to call back.

✦

The May holidays began. Kit told me he'd be going to Western Australia for a week. He asked if I was going anywhere, and I said, 'To the library.' But I didn't leave my flat. I'd get up in the morning, make coffee and porridge, refill my hot water bottle, and return to bed. I sat up against my pillows wrapped in a huge, pilled woollen shawl, and began reading Virginia Woolf's diary for the first time, stopping to shove my hands under the covers when they grew too cold to hold the book.

I had a five-volume paperback edition of the diary. The cover of each volume showed various personal items laid out on Woolf's desk. Now and then I'd interrupt my reading to gaze at them. Notebooks lying open provided glimpses of her handwriting. It occurred to me that those notebooks were probably the very diaries I was reading, and the realisation was thrilling. Woolf's spectacles were part of the array – the roundness of their lenses was especially touching. There was also a necklace made of shining, greeny-blue shells that looked as if they might have come from the Pacific. These intimate objects that Woolf had handled so often made a vibration in time, bringing her close.

I skipped the first two volumes of the diary because they weren't relevant to the novels I was writing about. Rather than reading the later volumes cover to cover, I used the index to locate entries pertinent to my work. I filled cards with useful notes. When I'd finished with Volume Five, I intended to read the whole diary through systematically, and so, one afternoon, having made myself a plate of Marie biscuits slathered with butter and Vegemite, I picked up Volume One.

I got to October 1917.

The air felt different after that.

'We came back to find Perera, wearing his slip & diamond initial in his tie as usual; in fact, the poor little mahogany coloured wretch has no variety of subjects. The character of the Governor, & the sins of the Colonial Office, these are his topics; always the same stories, the same point of view, the same likeness to a caged monkey, suave on the surface, inscrutable beyond. He made me uncomfortable by producing an e[n]velope of lace – "a souvenir from Ceylon Mrs Woolf" – more correctly a bribe, but there was no choice but to take it.'

A footnote to Woolf's entry for 16 October 1917 identified Perera as E. W. Perera. That was a name honoured in Sri Lanka; I'd learned why in school. In 1915 violent fighting had broken out in the British colony of Ceylon between Muslims and Sinhalese. The British authorities, jumpier than usual because of the war with Germany, had misread communal conflict as anti-imperial revolt. The governor declared martial law, 'Shoot on Sight' orders produced dozens of summary executions, and local leaders were imprisoned without cause.

A group of Ceylonese met in secret at E. W. Perera's house and drew up a memorandum to the British Secretary of State for the Colonies, detailing atrocities and pleading for the repeal of martial law. It was decided that Perera would carry the memorandum to London, a dangerous journey due to the threat of German submarines and mines on the shipping routes. He was chosen because he was a barrister and a Christian, which calmed the suspicions of the British authorities. They took him for a scholar rather than an activist, believed his story about wanting to carry out research in the British Museum, and granted him permission to travel. Perera boarded a ship with the memorandum sewn into his shoe. After its contents became known in London, the governor of the colony was recalled and the imprisoned Ceylonese leaders were released.

The British government asked the new governor to look into his predecessor's response to the riots. When his report came out, it was a whitewash. Perera, along with other prominent Ceylonese who'd joined him in England, now pressed for a more searching investigation.

Before Leonard Woolf married Virginia Stephen, he'd served in the colonial administration in Ceylon. He sympathised with Perera and his countrymen, and collaborated with them on how best to prosecute their case. They gained support among British MPs and in the left-wing press, but calls for a formal enquiry into the response to the riots were ignored, and the hoped-for debate in the House of Commons never took place.

My poster of Woolf was the famous photograph taken when she was young. It showed her in a white or pale-coloured dress with her body facing forward but her head turned to the right. Her long dark hair was drawn over the tops of her ears and coiled into a bun on her nape. She was glancing down, her lips slightly parted as if she were about to speak. I'd placed the image above my desk because I liked to imagine Woolf saying something encouraging as she watched me work.

Sitting at my desk as she presided over me that evening, I copied her diary entry for 16 October 1917 onto an index card. I wrote down a few other entries as well, all displaying morbid symptoms along similar lines. Then I tore the cards into small pieces and pushed them deep into the rubbish in my bin.

A little mahogany-coloured wretch got up in finery was delivered to a Woolf.

He performed.

She assessed.

No Distinction.

No Pass With Merit.
No Pass.

✦

Shaz rang to invite me to a gig, and I invented an excuse. The weather was appalling, and the world was going to end. Trams passed, sounding their bells. One screeched around a corner as I was falling asleep, and I thought there was a soul at my window. Plates piled up in the sink. Whenever I added to them, I thought of the poster in Anti's kitchen: 'After you've smashed the state, you'll still have to do the dishes.' Rubbish accumulated in my kitchen bin. Everyone had assured me there were no cockroaches in Melbourne, but my Sydney heart was certain that they were only in hiding, massing for attack.

Benedict rang for a natter. He was working on a book of linked short stories, he told me. The title was *Bildungstheorie*. I asked what that meant, and he said that the stories were about a teenager born into a homophobic family in New Zealand who builds his sense of self through Theory. 'Basically, it's a book about me.'

✦

The phone rang at night. The interstate beeps were neon signs flashing 'Mother' and 'Emergency'. Kit apologised for calling when it was so late in Melbourne. 'I went out for a run after dinner and spotted this phone box.' I asked how his holiday was going, and he said he'd rather be studying. It was a brief conversation because he soon ran out of coins.

One of the first things I'd noticed about Olivia was that her breasts were fuller than mine. I thought about Kit nuzzling those glamorous breasts in Western Australia. I thought, I can't keep abreast, ha ha. I thought, I should follow Kit's prescription for Liz, go down into the street, find a man, ask him up.

✦

In *A Room of One's Own*, published in 1929, Woolf writes, 'We think back through our mothers if we are women.' It's one of her most famous observations, enshrined in feminist thinking and giving off a quasi-religious glow.

I pondered what it might mean for a daughter to think back through her mother.

When Woolf was growing up, the tea table stood at the centre of her family's life. Every day her mother, Julia Stephen, presided over afternoon tea in the drawing room. Drawing-room tea was an aesthetic ritual and it called for a certain type of conversation: sparkling, flowing, light. Julia Stephen excelled at it. Watching her, her daughters absorbed the rules. After she died, her husband, Leslie, required the young women to take over their mother's role at the tea table. Virginia and her sister, Vanessa, grew to loathe this daily ceremony in their father's house, its prescribed manners, the constraining 'tea-table politeness' it imposed.

When Leslie Stephen died, in 1904, his daughters set up a scandalously loose new form of household, one in which categories came unfixed. Virginia and Vanessa drank coffee after dinner instead of tea and substituted toilet paper for starched table napkins. Under their roof, women and men talked together freely about everything, even sex.

But in 1917, a colonial preoccupied with imperial injustice showed up in Woolf's drawing room at teatime. His conversation, focused on politics, lacked the lightness and sparkle mandated for Victorian tea-table talk. He was mahogany-coloured, overdressed, and ill at ease, and Woolf's aversion to him was more powerful than her modernity. Recording his visit in her diary, she thought back through her mother as she wrote.

✦

Kit brought me a West Australian present of a tiny, clenched, white shell. We spent an afternoon, an evening, and a night together. Being with him again felt new as well as lovingly familiar – exciting and companionable at once.

✦

'I missed hearing your voice on Sunday but I understand that you had to unplug the phone to study undisturbed. Is your flat nice and warm? People say that Melbourne is very cold in winter but I suppose you have to put up with it as it is what you chose.'

✦

May ticked over into June. I'd have sworn that nothing had changed while Kit was away, but that couldn't have been the case. We spent a few more nights together, and then one morning I heard myself saying that I didn't want to see him again. Kit's face grew formal, but he didn't ask why. That was lucky, because the much-folded paper serviette that had come into my mind was hardly an explanation. We kissed tenderly for a long time before parting, but no one said, 'See you soon.' With my forehead against the door, I listened to his steps going down the stairs.

The green velvet curtain at my bedroom window was threadbare in places. The upper pane had been replaced by dimpled glass. On this brilliant morning, the walls were sun-spangled. The bed still remembered our animal smells. 'Be the one to break up. Be the one. Be the cool one.' I lay there as the air grew cold around me, feeling elderly and calm.

✦

The boarding house at the end of the street had a tall bay window on the ground floor. A woman with a nimbus of snowy hair often sat there, framed by orange curtains, looking out at the concrete yard. One day she was retrieving an envelope from the letterboxes near the gate as I was heading for the station. Her outfit caught my eye: chalk-blue jumper, red trousers, pink socks. Everything looked well worn, but the colours were symphonic. I offered a bright 'Good morning!' and a smile.

She was holding a typed envelope addressed to Mrs Pearl Walker. 'You Koori?' she asked, and turned away when I said no.

✦

The airless corridors of the English department smelled of photocopier and fear. Students were milling about a noticeboard, sniggering at a hand-drawn cartoon strip with three frames:

1. Happy student arrives at university clutching a teddy bear labelled 'Literature'.

2. Snarling tutor in a T-shirt labelled 'Theory' rips teddy to pieces.

3. Student sobs.

Paula said that she was hoping I had a draft chapter

for her. I'd been reading Woolf's diary, I said, and handed her my copy of Volume One. The machinery of racism ran silently in 1986. It was unmentionable, shameful and ordinary. How could I fit it into a sentence about Virginia Woolf? I couldn't even fit it into a sentence about myself.

Paula looked at the entries marked with Post-its, and I looked at my knees, or at Paula's poster of Woolf. It was the same as mine, but hers was framed and under glass. Paula handed back the diary, saying that of course Woolf was a terrible snob and unforgivably rude about colonials. She'd described Katherine Mansfield as common. 'Anyway, how's that chapter coming along?'

'I got caught up reading the diary.'

Background reading could easily become a dangerous vortex, Paula said. She urged me to get on and start writing. It was a question of balance: it was important not to focus on what came down to a very small fraction of the millions of words that Woolf produced. I pointed out that it was a very large fraction of what she'd produced about Ceylonese. I kept my voice soft and smiled widely to ask forgiveness for being the mahogany-coloured wretch in Paula's drawing room. Any minute, I'd be pulling out an envelope full of lace.

Paula swished her ringlets. 'That type of appalling thinking was everywhere at the time, of course. It's important to keep that in mind.'

I wanted to say that Leonard Woolf had usually managed to rise above that kind of appalling thinking, but I couldn't come up with the words.

'Take Woolf's anti-Semitism,' Paula continued. 'You'd have come across plenty of that in your reading. Plenty. She said, among other things, that she'd hated marrying a Jew, and she referred to her husband as "the Jew" in his presence. He didn't mind – he was used to that kind of thing. I've contextualised and historicised that aspect of Woolf, and now I've set it aside. Even though I'm Jewish.'

My surprise must have shown because she said that, to be completely accurate, her stepmother was Jewish. 'Mum died when I was a baby, so my stepmum is my mum, really.'

Paula went on to remind me that I'd chosen to write about three novels: *The Waves*, *The Years*, and *Between the Acts*. My thesis could mention what Woolf's diary had to say about the composition or reception of those works, but that was optional. 'Go back to the chapter breakdown you gave me. Focus on the fiction. You're working towards a Masters, not a PhD. All you have to do is fulfil the requirements of the university. No examiner will object if you bracket off the diary.'

She suggested that I give a paper in the department's postgraduate seminar series. It would provide me with a short-term deadline and an incentive to write.

Afterwards, in the library stacks, I alternated for a while between walking around to turn on pointless lights and standing very still until everything went dark.

When I left the library I ran into Amabel and her three-decades-older twin. Mops was English and had expensive hair. She was taking Amabel out to lunch. Amabel invited me to the salon that she hosted with Olivia on the first Saturday of each month. 'We've been practising a violin duet, and after that someone might recite a poem or read out something they've written. Last month a friend brought along a recording of Janet Baker singing "Where Corals Lie" – I don't suppose you know it, it's sublime. We always have a play reading to finish up. It's always Shakespeare, and everyone joins in. We're doing *As You Like It* next. I'm sure we can find you a small part.'

✦

The phone rang. When I answered, the caller hung up.

✦

I asked Anti if she'd read *A Room of One's Own*, and she asked if the pope shat in the woods. 'That book explained my life.'

'That's what I thought when I read it.'

'It explains the life of every woman on the planet.'

I asked Lenny if he'd read *A Room of One's Own*. He

said that Virginia Woolf was a product of the British upper middle class, and that her book was addressed to women like her. 'She knew nothing about working-class lives.'

I asked Shaz if she'd read *A Room of One's Own*. She said that it had changed her life. 'Virginia Woolf was like my mother if my mother had been like I wanted.'

I thought about her/my/our Woolfmother. She was our *Bildungstheorie*, showing us how to understand ourselves in relation to the world. Our mothers closed doors in order to keep us safe and never stopped warning us about the dangers outside. The Woolfmother said, 'Imagine!' and opened doors in our minds. She was the one we turned to when our own mothers failed. Our mothers failed because: (1) We were obliged to ignore them; (2) We kept presenting them with our pooey nappies; (3) They didn't have £500 a year and a room of their own in a Bloomsbury square.

The Woolfmother outed herself as a snob and a racist and an anti-Semite, failing us because mothers are obliged to fail. But her writing about women inspired us and gave us courage because *our imaginations were bigger than hers*. Our imaginations projected us into sentences intended for upper-middle-class Englishwomen. They propelled us into a future in which we were artists and scholars and our lives were experimental adventures. In that future we could destroy the Woolfmother, rip her to pieces, and end up motherless and weeping. Or we could frame her, put her up on a wall, and keep her under glass.

Theory had taught me wariness around either/or, so I came up with a different solution. Acknowledgement lay between denial and tearing down. Very carefully, I slid a table knife between the wall and the four blobs of Blu Tack holding up my poster of the Woolfmother. She came away undamaged from her location above my desk, and I repositioned her on the dark wall behind my front door. Now that she was cornered and her eyes were level with mine, her downcast gaze was that of a naughty child unable to look her parent in the face.

My bathroom was at the opposite end of the hallway. It didn't have an extractor fan, and the window was warped shut. Steam from my shower, escaping into the hall, kept unsticking the Woolfmother, but she always contrived to hang on by a corner or two.

◆

My index cards testified to current trends in Woolf scholarship. The French feminists adored her because her radically Maternal prose disrupted the Word of the Father and the Symbolic Order. The Anglo-American feminists adored her because she wrote women-centred fiction and theorised the material conditions of women's lives. Paula adored her because Paula needed a Major,

Undergraduate-Friendly Woman Writer for her first-year unit on Modernism. Gertrude Stein wasn't Undergraduate Friendly, and Sylvia Plath was Undergraduate Friendly to a problematic degree – in Sydney, where she'd featured on the syllabus, young women I knew produced passionate, alarming, footnote-free essays about 'Sylvia'.

Did Woolf's diary represent one self, while her fiction and essays represented another? If her diary expressed private thoughts and her books expressed public ones, did that mean that her diary self was the true one? Was there a hierarchy of Woolfish selves, and, if so, was one more profound/more authentic/higher/better than the other?

Also:

Why were we reading her private diary?

In her dazzling, image-making way, Woolf had a cascade of metaphors for her diary. It was a waste-paper basket. It was a bath into which she could sink. It was a pillow on which to weep. It was a laboratory for experimenting with style. It was a handkerchief on which she could rid herself of the mucus of depression ('Sneezing & blowing is better than incubating germs').

Another metaphor for a diary is a collection of morbid symptoms. Something momentous collapsed in Woolf's lifetime, too. She had to come up with new ways of being and of rendering that being in literature, and it was difficult and exciting. Her diary was what happened in the interregnum between the life she invented for herself, and her representation and theorising of women's lives in groundbreaking books. When the symptoms could no longer be contained by her diary, she waded into a river with her pockets full of stones.

If I kept a diary, it would overflow with morbid symptoms about Lois, for one.

If Lois, for one, read my diary, I was pretty sure that she wouldn't want to write a thesis about my work.

✦

As winter closed in, draughts that had flirted with icebergs slipped past my ill-fitting windows and ran through my rooms. Windy blasts from the Southern Ocean hurtled unopposed along the streets, their cold hair flowing. Joseph Brodsky calls rivers and streets 'the long things of life' – he'd have been right at home in Melbourne. Demonstrating perspective as they vanished into the distance, the city's endless, flat, unkinking streets made me feel as if they might draw me on forever. I wondered whether, if I stayed long enough, my thoughts would stretch, would unroll steadily, without hurry or fret about destination.

From my back door I had a view of distant, vertical glass. The towers along St Kilda Road tried to counter the wintry darkness with their vertiginous grids of light. In daylight hours their mirrored faces multiplied the clouds. Sydney was a place where the trees were scaled for dinosaurs, a place where deep time felt close. Melbourne seemed weightless: a modern mirage floating in the present tense.

✦

'Babs rang yesterday and talked a lot of rubbish. She is a Supervisor now, it seems. She invited me to lunch for her birthday but I don't know if I can be bothered. It's such a long way and the last time I went there I had an upset tummy afterwards. The eggplant was swimming in oil but you can't say anything to Babs. Her birthday is on the second of next month. Don't forget to send a card or I'll never hear the end of it.'

✦

Previously Olivia had struck me as nothing much to look at, but now I found myself haunted by the wide, strong planes of her face. It was a face that would photograph well, I saw. As for the colour of her hair, I'd have called it 'mustard', but the longer I considered it, the brighter it grew. Shakespeare had described it: 'My Lady's hair is threads of beaten gold.' He'd described mine too, the famous 'black wires'. No woman likes the sound of those, and we've never believed Shakespeare did either. I closed my eyes and saw Olivia's hair turn into a halo, brilliant with gold leaf. I found the right word for it: 'glory'. She was going about her days shrouded in glory, a beautiful woman with milky skin.

After sending Kit away, I didn't shower for two days. I put off taking my sheets to the laundromat, and when I did, and they came out of the dryer smelling only of warm lemons, it felt like defeat. But Olivia, not Kit, was the one I kept thinking about. Sometimes she was navigating tram tracks on her bike and sometimes she was playing the piano and sometimes she was smiling at a camera held by Kit. Mainly she was displacing Lois as the focal point of my morbid symptoms.

✦

The neon Coca-Cola sign at St Kilda Junction was replaced by one for Foster's. Benedict read this as a heartening shift from the global to the local, but Lenny dismissed it as just another symptom of Late Capitalism's 'creative-destructive energies'. Benedict, who looked as if he lived on air, had a fathomless appetite, and was shovelling in a double serving of eggs and bacon at the Galleon. The rest of us were getting stuck into spanakopitas around our sparkly red table, and Lenny kept us entertained with grim remarks about advertising discourse and its interpellation of the consumer.

Benedict had brought a friend along that day. Some years later, when I saw a trailer for *The Lover*, the film based on Marguerite Duras's novel, I thought at first that it starred Maeve. She was studying dance and drama when we met, and she spoke about chakras with a small, intent frown. It was Saturday lunchtime, and the Galleon was packed. Customers coming and going would catch sight of Maeve, look away, look again in awed tribute to her face.

✦

I decided to grow my hair.

✦

Kit lived in the dreary stretch of Carlisle Street between Barkly Street and Brighton Road. That July I took to walking past his building at evening rush hour, when the air smelled of seaweed and exhaust, hoping to see Olivia making her way to his flat. Anxious not to miss her, I searched for a bright head in the swarm of commuters hurrying home. I couldn't be sure which tram she'd have caught – she might even have taken the Punt Road bus – so I kept turning around and hurrying back the way I'd come.

I'd once written a lengthy essay on Shelley's 'The Triumph of Life'. I remembered his vision of a great stream of rushing people, each one hastening along without really knowing where they were headed, 'numerous as gnats'. The poem contained a south wind and icy cold and the glare of desire, and all these correspondences with my surroundings and my wishes confirmed the rightness of my presence in the street. 'A cold bright car with savage music', I quoted to myself as a lighted tram rollicked past.

✦

I started obsessing about the red shirt Olivia had worn to Leo's. 'Where can I find a shirt with an open collar that lies flat?' I asked Anti. 'I don't like the standard kind that sticks up.'

Anti looked me over. 'That's because you have a short torso and long legs. A collar that buttons up high hides your throat and shortens your top half further. You need something open there, to create length. No turtlenecks for you, baby. Also you should stay away from high-rise waists, but if you've gone and bought a skirt or pants like that, *don't* tuck in your top – your tits will end up on your belt.'

It was jaw-dropping! 'All the stuff I've avoided because it makes me look weird. You've just explained why.'

Anti rose and struck a diva pose. 'That's the purpose of art,' she said grandly. 'It gives form to experience. It makes sense of our lives.'

We were drinking coffee in her studio in Prahran, where Anti was working towards a new show made up of enormous images on sheets of taped-together butcher paper. She'd drawn on the sheets with charcoal, then smudged or erased her lines, and drawn over them again. The blurry results were hallucinatory. I saw interiors and facades, caryatids, blind archways, tilted columns, stairs that led nowhere. Vaulted, shadowy spaces contained forms that resembled engines and pulleys and other powerful machines. Faces looked out through a barred window, or they might have been outside, peering in. A train stood at a station where people in hats and long heavy coats were waiting on the platform. Images that originated in reality but transcended it, they suggested half-repressed memories, or dreams.

The series was called *Junta*, Anti said. 'All the murdering, military shits everywhere and their death machinery. Greece, obviously, but also Argentina, Chile.'

Hands on hips, she was moving slowly around the studio, gazing up at her work. 'All this has been inside me, struggling to get out, for years. I had to give it expression. I had to find it a form. It's strong work.' She turned to me, her face lively with thinking. 'Now I'm through with history painting. I'm going to focus on making art that doesn't look like art. Art that has the feel of women talking everyday crap, like you and me here, me solving all your problems . . .'

I mimed punching her, but I was thinking of my awed reaction to Gillian Leahy's film about Liz's/my life: 'I didn't know that this could be art.'

✦

My mother was gleeful on the phone. At Easter she'd collected her neighbours' mail while they were away, and by way of thanks had received a green shot-silk scarf. My mother loathed green, believing it to be unlucky. For instance: against her advice, my father had bought a shirt with green checks, and guess what he'd been wearing when he received his diagnosis? Now my mother had given – 'palmed off' – the scarf to my aunt for her birthday. With a single stroke she'd saved the cost of a present and given her sister bad luck.

I asked how my aunt had reacted to the scarf.

'Oh, she was thrilled! Thrilled to the marrow,' said my mother in a voice divided between triumph and scorn. Then she told me off for having missed my aunt's birthday and made me promise to send a Belated Greetings card.

My mother's dislike of green had been passed down from her mother, who might have received it from her mother in turn. I have no idea how my aunt had escaped. Another thing I knew was that, if my mother misbehaved when she was a child, my grandmother would say, 'Your father won't like you as much as your sister.'

My mother went on to say she'd discovered a tie that had belonged to my father at the back of a drawer. My father and the Woolfmother's father were both called Leslie, a tiny, pleasing link, like Leonard Woolf's connection with Ceylon. My mother had always called my father Les, but now she said 'Less', pronouncing his name with a drawn-out hiss. I corrected her. She ignored me. She was wondering whether to offer the tie to her sister's husband. 'I bought that tie for Less. It cost a lot of money and it's like new.'

'Lezz.' I raised my voice. '*Lezz.*'

'Why are you shouting? Don't shout.'

'You mean you bought the tie for Lezz.'

'That's what I'm telling you.' She sounded bewildered. 'It's the tie I got Less just before he got ill.'

Sometime after I moved out of home, my mother had begun to refer to the women's magazines she bought each week as books. In the same way, when I graduated and began working, she'd refer to 'your market research shop'. It was useless to tell her that I worked in an office, as she did. I realised that Less was another of these mysterious locutions. Before she rang off, she said it again. My father had become Less.

✦

I told Lenny about Woolf's description of E. W. Perera. He said it was a pity I hadn't chosen to work on, say, Salman Rushdie. 'Postcolonial studies is a significant new field.'

'Paula wouldn't want to supervise that. She doesn't know the area – women's writing is her thing.'

The reason under that reason was the time I'd wanted to take Spanish as an extra subject at school. I needed permission from Mr Richardson, the Year 10 coordinator, and he asked why I didn't learn Indonesian or Japanese instead. 'Wouldn't an Asian language be more suitable for someone of your background?'

I thought that it would be more suitable still for someone of Mr Richardson's background to learn Indonesian or Japanese.

The reason under that reason was my reluctance to tear down the Woolfmother.

I kept renewing her Blu Tack.

I kept answering my mother's calls.

✦

In Woolf's autobiographical essay 'Sketch of the Past', she writes: 'I still shiver with shame at the memory of my half-brother, standing me on a ledge, aged about six or so, exploring my private parts.' The half-brother she's referring to is Gerald Duckworth, who was seventeen or eighteen when the abuse took place.

Later in the same essay, Woolf writes about her other half-brother, George: 'It was usually said that he was father and mother, sister and brother in one – and all the old ladies of Kensington and Belgravia added with one accord that Heaven had blessed those poor Stephen girls beyond belief and it remained for them to prove that they were worthy of such devotion [. . .] The old ladies of Kensington and Belgravia never knew that George Duckworth was not only father and mother, brother and sister to those poor Stephen girls; he was their lover also.'

No one knows exactly when George Duckworth began sexually abusing the Stephen girls. It might have begun after their mother's death, when Woolf was thirteen. What's clear from her testimony is that it was taking place when she was eighteen and George was thirty-two.

In his biography of Woolf, her nephew Quentin Bell observes, 'In later years Virginia's and Vanessa's friends were a little astonished at the unkind mockery, the downright virulence, with which the sisters referred to [George].'

When Woolf was in her fifties, she still remembered 'resenting, disliking' what George did when he climbed into her bed. She asks, 'What is the word for so dumb and mixed a feeling? It must have been strong, since I still recall it.'

Dumb, mixed feelings are knowledge that lives outside language and outside time. Learning that George has died, Woolf writes in her diary, '[H]ow childhood goes with him – the batting, the laughter, the treats, the presents, taking us for bus rides to see famous churches, giving us tea at City Inns'. Now that he's dead, her resentment and dislike can safely mingle with affection for the kindly older brother of her early years.

Elsewhere she calls him 'God, faun and pig'.

The Reason Under All The Reasons for not tearing down the Woolfmother: our mutual shiver of shame.

✦

'I know you would have acknowledged the parcel straight away so it must not have reached you yet. I went to the post office in my lunch break and asked them about it, and the man in charge said he was not aware of any strikes or delays here or in Melbourne. I am afraid it must have been lost or stolen. I should have sent it registered but it didn't occur to me at the time. As soon as I saw that shade of pink I knew it would suit you. The wool is 8-ply Paton's Totem, which is a good brand and not cheap. The jumper has raglan sleeves and I put a lot of work into knitting it. It is awful to think of it being lost.'

✦

I dialled Olivia's number. 'Hal-*lo*?' It sounded like Mops. I hung up.

✦

I told Anti about Woolf's description of E. W. Perera. I said that, although I'd been transfixed by *Midnight's Children*, I didn't want to write about Rushdie or anyone else. 'No other writer has meant as much to me as Woolf. I've been reading her books and thinking about them since I was at school.'

Anti mulled over this for a while. Then, 'You know what, though? Didn't Rushdie say that thing about the empire writing back? You could find inspiration there.' She had Aristotle's categorisation of human activities in mind, she said. 'He distinguishes *theoria*, which increases knowledge, from *praxis*, which is action-for-itself. In between those two comes *poiesis*, which is action-for-making. *Poiesis* is creative. Make a film, paint, write a poem. Write back to Woolf.'

✦

Paula and Myron were standing together outside the campus bookshop. She was looking up at him, laughing and nodding while he held forth. I was on my way to have lunch in a pub with a medievalist called Elise. She organised the postgraduate seminars, was doing a PhD on *Piers Plowman*, and turned out to be an excellent source of departmental gossip. Over fried camembert with cranberry sauce, I learned that Theory had arrived in the department with the appointment of Myron to the professorial chair. The Leavisites in charge at the time had misread Myron as a harmless Milton scholar from Cornell with impressive credentials. But Myron had sworn a blood oath to Theory and would go on to ensure that every subsequent hire had done the same. A few broken Leavisites continued to occupy the smaller, dingier offices, but only in a wistful 'Is there sherry still for tea?' kind of way.

Elise also said that a tenured lectureship was coming up in English at the end of the year. 'There are three lecturers on contracts and they're all after it. The department should appoint Paula, really, she publishes heaps, but Myron wants Guy. Have you come across Guy? He's an Althusserian Marxist.'

'Is that a Marxist who strangles their class enemies?'

'Going by my sample of one, it's a Marxist with an E-Type Jag.'

I told Elise about seeing Paula with Myron, and she said that pretend-laughing with senior academics was an essential workplace skill we should be allowed to list on our CVs. She also told me that Paula had once published a blistering review of a debut novel written by a woman. The novel was unfeminist, according to Paula, and the novelist had betrayed women by depicting a female protagonist who was moping about the end of an affair. 'The thing is, everyone knows that Paula's boyfriend left her for this writer not long before the book came out. This stuff happened five, six years ago, and the writer hasn't published anything since.'

Elise sat back in her chair, raising and lowering her circumflex eyebrows and beaming. She urged me to attend the fortnightly staff research seminars. 'They're a hoot. Last time there was this lovely, sincere woman visiting from somewhere like Hull. She was wearing academic slacks, she spoke really illuminatingly about her life's work on Keats, and she didn't mention De Man or Bloom or *any* Theory even once. At the end of her paper there was horrified silence for a bit, and then Guy pushed up his sunnies and asked one of those questions that means, Do you realise that Everything You Have Said Is Wrong? My name for the staff seminars is Lions and Christians. You really should come along. The department puts on wine and cheese and cabana afterwards, it's all disgusting, but at least you get fed.'

✦

On Friday night a bunch of us were at the Prince of Wales to hear Says Ann. Between sets, Lenny told me about a woman who'd called the helpline. 'Her husband runs a hardware shop in South Gippsland. He's dying. He's told her everything, she knows he's been fucking men for years. She says she doesn't care. She loves him and wants to look after him. No one in the town will go near them, so she rings the helpline just to talk. I told her she was the bravest and kindest person I knew.'

Later Benedict and Lenny got ready to head off with backpacks of leaflets. They'd hit the clubs, distributing information about AIDS testing and safe sex. A guy whose name I've forgotten asked if they danced as well or just handed out leaflets to the queues. Benedict sighed gustily. 'Mate. Are we not *poofters*?' He assumed that Disco John Travolta pose. 'We *always* make time to dance.'

✦

The Woolfmother had fallen off the wall when I got home, and I trod on her in the dark. I was just smashed enough to call Kit. He answered on the seventh ring. I'd intended to hang up but said, 'Feel like studying?' Because oh, I really did. He hung up. As if all the walls between us had turned to glass, I watched him walk away from the phone. 'Wrong number,' he told

Olivia, although she hadn't asked. He pissed noisily in the bohemian bathroom that she'd cleaned that afternoon and returned to bed.

Kit always fell asleep easily. I took pleasure in the thought of Olivia lying awake, neat as a corpse, straining to catch the name Kit muttered as he fought the bedclothes, now and then fingering her golden heart.

✦

At my desk, with the lamp on and my dollar-swallowing heater scorching my ankles, I built a fortification of index cards covered in notes. I took the lid off my typewriter, inserted a sheet of paper, and summoned Paula.

Focus on the fiction.

Bracket off.

Write.

Each ten thousand words Woolf produced was a mattress. Not the thin Japanese kind but mattresses stuffed with the feathers of plump English geese.

I lay on top of the towering heap of mattresses, wriggling to get comfortable.

Contextualised, historicised, set aside under the tower: a pea-size, mahogany-coloured wretch.

Wriggle.

Wriggle.

Wriggle.

I climbed off the mattresses and into my bed.

✦

Lenny mentioned that Maeve and he had gone to the Galleon on the weekend and found Kit and Olivia already there, having lunch. The following Saturday I kept glancing at the door, waiting for the two of them to arrive. They'd join our table, and Olivia would take off her jumper and sit beside Kit in her red shirt, her woven hair shining like her heart. I realised that I couldn't bear the sight of her sitting beside Kit in her red shirt, with her woven hair and her heart. I made an excuse and left without ordering lunch.

✦

Amabel was heading away from uni, coatless although the wind was bitter. I followed her all the way to Fitzroy, swinging my arms as she did, claiming space. Eventually she turned into a narrow street. I was just in time to see her entering a house with a bright red door in a two-storey bluestone terrace.

Back on Brunswick Street, I made my way towards a tram stop, pausing to scrutinise windows. I was eyeing the mannequins in a vintage clothing place when a voice cried, 'Hal-*lo*!' Mops asked if I'd been visiting

'Bel and Liv'. I managed to look puzzled, and she told me that they lived just around the corner. 'We bought ourselves an inner-city pied-à-terre for those nights when we finish up late at work. And the girls use it now, which is just perfect.'

The wind was making my eyes water, but Mops wasn't through. She asked how long I'd lived in Australia. 'We're immigrants, too,' she said. 'We came out in '64. In fact my husband's family came to England from Barcelona when he was a baby, so he's an immigrant twice over. Bel was born here – she's a real Aussie.'

She told me that her gallery was only a few blocks along and encouraged me to drop in. I accepted the business card that she produced from a garment as ashy and architectural as her hair.

✦

I went on with secondary reading for my seminar paper, which would discuss Woolf's late bestseller, *The Years*. After her revolutionary experiments in modernism, Woolf had set out to write a different kind of novel. It would alternate between essays and fiction: between 'fact and vision', as she called it, between the 'granite' of truth and the 'rainbow' of character. The mix of fact and fiction was to be 'a fresh form'. The fiction would track the evolution of British social politics by showing the changing lives of Woolf's characters, and the essays would discuss the difficulty, for a woman, of writing a new kind of novel. But as Woolf grappled with the exigencies of writing, the idea of interleaving fiction and polemic fell away, and she rewrote the 'novel-essay' she'd begun as fiction. When *The Years* was finished, its marked interest in public life was the sole trace of Woolf's original plan.

The novel began in the Victorian age and tracked the fortunes of the Pargiters, an upper-middle-class English family, over half a century. The Pargiter daughters were called Eleanor, Delia, Milly, and Rose. I wondered, not for the first time, why my parents, Leslie and Jean, had given me a name that signified Common and Dumb. I asked my mother. Full of indignation, she said, 'It's a lovely name!' It was a modern name, free of family associations, so that might have been why my father and mother, each named for a parent, had chosen it for me.

We came from a country where names served primarily to identify ethnicity. My mother didn't grasp that in Australia they functioned as markers of class. Australia was committed to denying the existence of social classes, so I hadn't grasped it either until I started doing market research. One of the directors read the London *Times* every day. When I arrived for the evening shift, I'd rescue the paper from his bin and apply myself to the cryptic crossword at quiet moments. These occurred early in a shift, when we were filling our demographic quotas with ease. Later we'd hunch over our phones, frantically dialling numbers generated at random and listed on a spreadsheet. Males aged fifty-five and over, rarely keen on talking to strangers, were always the most difficult category to fill. In the last half-hour of the shift, I'd make up their replies for them and enter invented phone numbers on their answer sheets – all the researchers did the same and no one ever checked.

Leafing through the *Times* one evening, I came across the social pages. The British were unabashed about the existence of social classes, and after studying those pages, I understood why I was the only person I'd met at university with my name. I understood why I'd never read a novel written by a woman with my name. And I understood why I'd never come across a character with my name in a novel: being Common and Dumb, a woman with my name couldn't possibly have an interior life.

In the chapter breakdown of my thesis that I'd prepared for Paula, my discussion of *The Years* focused on the progress of feminism as represented in the emancipatory trajectory of the Pargiter women over the course of their lives. But that was before I had to reckon with a mahogany-coloured wretch. These days he'd grown large and bold and taken up squatting on a corner of my desk. I began to see the new direction my paper would take.

✦

In Kit's street that evening rain was falling, Melbourne's thin, spiteful winter rain. I decided to walk briskly up to Brighton Road, return along the opposite side of the street and go home. Near the intersection, hoping to spot Olivia on her way to see Kit, I almost walked into him. I stared, too startled to speak. He must have thought that I hadn't recognised him, because he pushed back the hood of his raincoat, saying, 'It's me.' His hair had been brutally cut. I said boldly that I'd been hoping to bump into him sometime. 'You said you'd teach me to ride a bike. I still want to learn.'

We arranged to meet in the park on Fitzroy Street on Sunday afternoon. On Saturday evening I went to Collingwood for Elise's birthday party. We bopped around her lounge room, sharing a joint. When the mixtape played 'Tainted Love', we belted it out. The track ended, and Elise said, 'There's always someone that song is about.'

At the party I met Reza from The Hague, who was visiting Australia for work. He told me that Persian was woefully deficient in obscenities, and that the worst insult you could offer a speaker of the language was to call him a sheep. I went back to his place. He drove me to St Kilda the next day, and we had lunch at the Galleon. No one I knew was there. We exchanged phone numbers, but I turned down his offer of a lift to my flat.

Everyone knows there are two types of mirrors, merciless and kind. The one over my bathroom sink was merciless, and I tried never to catch sight of myself in it. The ancient wardrobe that the previous tenant had left in the bedroom had one short leg propped up with a book, but its long oval mirror was forgiving. I lingered in front of its muffled light that afternoon, rejoicing in the power of my naked, mahogany-coloured body, with which I could do as I liked.

Kit arrived at the park on a woman's bike. It belonged to one of his neighbours, he said. 'It just sits there in the garage, so I asked if I could borrow it.' He explained about brakes, as wind pulled the clouds apart, blueing the sky. Space opened in my chest in response. How immense the world was, how blue and arched! It filled me with staggering joy. I practised sitting astride the bike with my toes touching the ground, and squeezing the brakes. After a while I pedalled slowly down the path, with Kit holding on to the seat to steady the heavy old frame. He reminded me to keep looking straight ahead, and then he let go. I fell off. I fell sideways onto the grass, and the bike fell on top of me, slamming into my knee.

Eventually I could wobble along for a few metres before hastily applying the brakes. It was a question of balance. Kit said that I was doing well, and needed only to practise. The clouds were returning, moving in from the bay like sharks, and we agreed to call it a day. Kit's neighbour had said that I could hang on to the bike for the present, and he urged me to take up her offer. 'Actually, I'm pretty sure she'd let it go for a few bucks if you wanted to buy it.' The problem, I pointed out, was that my building didn't have anywhere to store a bike. 'I'll have to keep it inside my flat,' I concluded doubtfully. Kit offered to give me a hand with getting it upstairs.

We headed past St Kilda Station into the full force of the wind. Kit had tied his jumper around his waist, and his checked shirt puffed out behind him and blew flat against his chest. A woman was coming the other way, pushing a stroller with a baby whose knitted arms ended in pink stars. We stepped aside, and the woman smiled her thanks, looking from my face to Kit's. It was obvious that she took us for a couple. For a frightening moment I saw how opaque other people's lives really are, but I went on believing that I could see into them all the same.

The bike seemed to fill my hallway, leaning against a wall. Kit stayed, of course. He had a T-shirt on underneath his shirt, the first time I'd seen him with an extra layer against the cold. When he was inside me, I told myself that he'd probably been with Olivia that morning, just as Reza had been with me. Again I was seized by savage joy.

I slept badly and woke with a sore knee. But there

was the surprise and happiness of waking up next to Kit. 'The triumph of life,' I repeated silently, lying against him in my warm bed.

When I returned from the kitchen with coffee, Kit was already getting dressed. His T-shirt was maroon and raggedly crenellated around the neck. Without looking at me, he said, 'You fucking anyone else?' It was the first time he hadn't said 'studying'. I almost said yes, I was, I wasn't waiting around for him, but instead I set his mug down and said, 'Aren't you?' in an equally belligerent tone.

'Have you had an AIDS test?' He scratched the top of his nose with the back of his thumbnail and concentrated on an inside-out sock.

'Why don't you use condoms?'

He looked up then, and his face ran with anger. Between gulps of coffee, he said he had to get going, he had an early tute. But when he was leaving, we kissed as tenderly as ever, and his hand found its way between my legs for a farewell caress. He liked to leave me like that, aroused, and to go away with my smell on his fingers. 'See you soon?' He formulated it as a question, which was yet another first.

✦

I spent a few more nights at Reza's place and hoped that Kit would come around or call while I was away.

If he did, he didn't mention it. He was showing up on random evenings now, and not as often or for as long as before. He'd arrive late, around nine, and leave early the next day without showering.

Reza went back to the Netherlands, and I missed falling asleep to soft jazz, and the strong, thick coffee he prepared on the hob. But it was a mild, almost pleasant nostalgia, rather than sadness.

✦

Lenny liked to rail against Now time, the Now-Now-Now that fostered consumerism, beating under Late Capitalism like a mechanical pulse. Sex was a different kind of Now time, archetypal time, time as timeless sensation. In reducing Lawrence to mince, Paula had let fall a raw, juicy scrap from one of the critical essays published after his death: 'The magnificent here and now of life in the flesh is ours, and ours alone, and ours only for a time.' I became ravenous in my pursuit of life in the flesh with Kit. Driving my frenzies was the wish to obliterate Olivia, to blast her from his mind. The minute he buzzed, I'd unlock my door, strip off, and be waiting in bed. I'd have torn at him as soon as he stepped inside, but the bike was in the way, besides which it was too cold to undress in the hall.

I no longer cared what marks I left on Kit. Let Olivia see! Let her read the deconstruction of their relationship on his flesh! I sucked on him, sank my nails into him. When he was out of the room, I liked to wipe myself with his clothing. Let her smell me! Let her smell us deconstructing her love!

When getting undressed Kit would lean forward, grab his windcheater or T-shirt by the back of the neck and pull it over his head. As he was completing this manoeuvre one day, I saw a dark, snaky hair on his grey jumper. I was Thrilled to the Marrow – it must have come off my carpet.

He left my place with a bruise developing on his chest. The next time I saw him he had a bruise on his neck. Olivia and I were exchanging messages about possession and power. Kit was only the paper on which we were writing to each other.

✦

I rang Elise to ask if staff attended the postgraduate seminars. I couldn't rid my mind of Everything You Have Said Is Wrong. Elise said that usually a student would invite their supervisor, but apart from that there were only postgrads present and everyone was very supportive. 'By the way, you missed a brilliant Lions and Christians last week. Guy was giving the paper, and he stopped after a while and apologised, saying that the next bit was really complex and he didn't expect anyone to follow. You should have seen Myron's face! And he couldn't have a go at Guy at question time because Guy's his guy. I was up the back practically wetting myself trying not to laugh.'

'What was the paper about?'

'Guy's self-enchantment, I believe.'

✦

I was entertaining a strong fantasy about breaking into the Fitzroy pied-à-terre after dark. There was certain to be a laneway behind that terrace. I'd wait until Amabel and Olivia had gone out one evening, and then I'd climb over their back fence. The kitchen window would be open at the bottom, or there'd be a key under a potted plant, something like that; in any case I'd find my way in. Once inside I'd cut up Olivia's clothes. I'd put one shoe from each pair into a bag and dump them in street bins on the way home.

Later I revised my plan. It would be creepier to emulate her jewellery ghost. I'd steal a belt from a coat, remove a button or two from shirts, slit some seams. Mysterious unravellings would appear in a few of Olivia's jumpers. I'd find the drawer or chest where she kept her summer clothes, introduce several inexplicable nicks and stains, and put everything back exactly as Olivia had stored it away. Then I'd lie on her bed, leaving a head-shaped indentation on her pillow when I rose. I plotted dozens of tiny, unnerving mysteries. Pages of notes gone from her folders. One sock missing from each pair.

✦

The bike remained in my hallway, where I kept banging my shin on a pedal. I'd progressed to riding cautiously in the park. I told my mother that I'd learned to ride a bike, knowing it would alarm her, and she said that if I fell off, I'd break all my teeth.

Whenever I tried to imagine introducing my mother to Mops or Amabel or Olivia or the horse semen heiresses, it made me shiver. Men were charmed by my plump, pretty mother. Raised to flatter them and defer to their opinions, she threw herself into the part. She'd left school at fifteen, which was the extent of the education her family could afford. All my catastrophic scenarios about her featured women. I feared their intelligence and their sparkling tea-table conversation and their diary entries describing her as common. It was my duty to shield her from them. No one else was allowed to punish her – she was mine alone.

✦

Kit had started mentioning Olivia now and then. He couldn't quite bring himself to say her name, but would come out with something like, 'We went out to Dights Falls on Saturday and got soaked in that downpour when we were riding back.' He preferred to make these statements while his head was still encased in whatever garment he was removing. He was trying to keep the truth in plain view, and was unable to show himself at the same time. Whenever this happened, I'd exact revenge by stealing coins or a low-denomination note from his wallet – nothing he could be sure he hadn't spent.

Kit ran his hand down my body, saying he'd had no idea skin could be so satiny and soft. This paying of compliments, too, was new. He said that I moved 'with a dancer's grace'. Another time, he said that he'd like to photograph me in the shirt I'd just put on. I felt jubilant. I'd spent a week's rent on that shirt – wave blue, it had a flat, open collar, and shell buttons a delicate, dawn-horizon colour between opal and pearl.

✦

Sometimes I thought of Reza. He had strong feelings about pizza and clouds. He sent me a postcard saying he'd never forget the way I sneezed. Would Kit remember anything about me? Reza was a kindly, humorous man, a good listener, interested only in whoever was speaking and what was being said. None of the things I liked about him applied to Kit. That was of no importance – why?

✦

'We' were taking Amabel to see *A Room with a View* because it was her birthday. That evening I caught a tram to Fitzroy, armed with a tote, disposable gloves, scissors, a packet of razor blades, and stuff for making stains. Olivia's street was a short one, and when I got there I saw that its single street light was nowhere near the pied-à-terre. But lights were shining inside the house, downstairs.

I walked around the block, thinking. Why had I assumed that 'we' would be taking Amabel to an early session of the film and out to dinner after that? 'We' might just as easily have decided to have dinner at home first. The temperature was dropping, and the only other person out and about in the back streets was a man with a hospital-white face and a football beanie who was walking his dog. I wished I had a beanie. I couldn't keep hanging around in the cold, but I didn't want to spend money in a pub. Back on Brunswick Street, a tram heading north, to Preston, was approaching. I hailed it at the stop.

My parents never went to parent-teacher nights, but once my mother and I had bumped into my maths teacher in a shopping centre. She was in a rush, she said, because she was going to visit her sister and had to get across the city to Rose Bay. My mother said, 'That's where rich people live.' The teacher laughed it off, saying all kinds of people lived there, you'd be surprised. I berated my mother for the rest of the day, repeating in cold fury that she'd come across as vulgar – *vulgar!* – and rude and ignorant, and how could she not know that it wasn't acceptable to talk about other people's financial status?

On the tram, I could think of nothing but other people's financial status. My family had sold everything to pay our airfares to Australia. The exchange rate took care of what savings were left. We'd arrived in Sydney with our suitcases and a few hundred dollars, grateful to be there. We'd never heard of the Assisted Migration Scheme, whereby white immigrants to Australia, the majority of whom were British, paid bargain-bin fares. In 1964 the scheme, a key component of the White Australia policy, was still intact. That was the landscape behind Mops's breezy 'We're immigrants, too.' Staring at my reflection in the window of the tram, I pictured her sauntering down a gangway, her pockets stuffed with sterling, and faceless Pobby, that 'immigrant twice over', treading close behind. The White Australia policy had been dismantled, but its legacy of racism was going strong. It ran hand in hand with Late Capitalism's commitment to wealth inequality. No doubt the pied-à-terre would be crammed with artworks and rugs and musical instruments and tasteful furniture and books. I resolved that, once inside, I'd smash a few splendid objects. I'd leave a bloody lipstick scrawl on a mirror: 'You Are Not Me!'

The tram reached its terminus, and I remained in my seat. The conductor winked as he punched my travel card for the return trip: 'Smart way to stay warm, love.' Long before we'd trundled back to Fitzroy, I understood that I'd never break into anyone's house. I intended to stay on the tram all the way home to St Kilda, and can't explain why I rose abruptly and tugged on the bell cord at the pied-à-terre stop. As I prepared to step off, the conductor called, 'Good night!', and I responded with a cheery wave.

The front of Olivia's place was in darkness now, so I went around to the lane. Lights showed in the back rooms of several houses. I halted by Olivia's fence, looking up at curtained French windows, outlined in light, that gave onto a small balcony. There was a smell of woodsmoke and bins. Somewhere close at hand a dog barked and kept on barking. I returned to the street.

A shadow detached itself from a lightless veranda a few doors along from the pied-à-terre. 'Can I help you?' asked the man, staring at my tote and then at my face. His beanie was familiar: it was the dog-walker. I muttered that I was just walking around, and he said there'd been quite a few break-ins in the area lately and that I should consider walking around somewhere else. 'For your own safety.'

The timetable at the stop informed me that I had twenty-three minutes to wait, so I set off towards the city, hoping to pick up a different tram. At the Rob Roy Hotel I turned around and saw Beanie Man standing at the top of his street, watching until he could be sure I was gone.

✦

'The jumper fits you very well but why have you tilted your head in the photo? Some people might think you had struck a pretty pose but I distinctly remember you telling me that the Osteopath said you should always hold your head straight.'

✦

I asked Kit what he'd thought of *A Room with a View*. He said that Amabel had woken up with a cold, so 'we' had baked her a cake and celebrated at home instead.

✦

Shaz marched into the Galleon, spectacular in pale pink crimplene and a red satin bomber jacket. Her ponytail had gone, leaving her skull covered in ragged silver tufts. The Danish waitress saw her and cried, 'Your hair is really wow!'

Shaz never pulled out a chair, scraping it on the floor, but lifted it away from the table instead. That day her face had the private, engrossed look it wore on stage, but without the joy. She lit a cigarette with the Bic she kept in the packet and told us that two days earlier she'd been walking home from a friend's place after dark, when a man grabbed her by her ponytail and dragged her into a lane. Her shouts brought a passer-by, and her assailant took off. 'First thing when I got home I chopped off my ponytail. Then I took a razor to the rest.'

Lenny's red face had turned white and slowly back to red. He asked if she'd been to the cops.

'Yesterday. I wasn't up to it at the time. The bloke who helped me didn't want anything to do with cops. He's a junkie. Anyway, neither of us got a good look at the prick who wanted to rape me. No chance he'll be identified.' Shaz ashed her cigarette and glared. 'You know the best bit? One of the cops was a woman. At the end of the interview she said, "What do you expect? You look like a prostitute."'

'Hope you reported her,' said Lenny at once.

'Are you fucking kidding? St Kilda cops! How long do you think before they pick me up in the street and "find" enough smack on me to charge me with dealing?'

✦

Kit had handed in an assignment that he felt confident would receive a high mark. The wind was throwing a tantrum that night, but the weather between us gentled. We ate cheese toasties sitting up companionably in bed. I told him about Paris, which I'd visited for the first time the previous year. I didn't say that I was lonelier there than I'd imagined was possible. The January sky was the colour of tin. 'The middle of winter', an expression I'd used lightly, revealed its full, vindictive sense: the middle of darkness, the middle of cold. I talked instead about things that time and distance had rendered 'bohemian': the zinc-topped counters in cafes, the bookstalls beside the river, my no-star hotel room with its square of hard towel and yellowing nylon sheets.

Paris looked as old as snow. Snow fell briefly on my first day there and never again. Determined not to yield to jet lag, I'd gone out walking. I was on the boulevard Arago, the long, blank stretch beside La Santé prison, when the snow began. Looking up, I saw a bare foot high in the air, on the other side of the wall. A prisoner on the top floor had stuck his foot through the bars of his cell and was waving it around in the snowy flakes.

I told Kit that I'd intended to get myself a couple of the ceramic bowls which the French used for milky coffee, but had never got around to buying them. He said that was a shame. I could see him picturing the bowls, finding them 'bohemian'. I knew that he was planning to visit his sister Meg in London at the end of the year, and now he said that he'd like to see Paris as well. I discouraged him at once, saying that the French were merciless to foreigners who didn't speak French. Also, Paris was scarily expensive. Why not go to Italy, I suggested, stroking his arm. It would be warmer there in every sense.

I assumed, of course, that he'd be travelling with Olivia. Paris was my place, and the thought of him discovering it with her made my chest go tight. Late one afternoon they'd take the lift to the top of the Eiffel Tower. I could see it: there they stood, hand-holding figurines on a wedding cake, daylight going, clusters and lines of street lights coming on below. The air smelled of petrol, and the hard, cheerless city was vanishing in the navy-blue distance. Why not go to Italy, I babbled – sumptuous, lemony Italy with its paintings and lakes? I longed to see it, I insisted, and he should do so. Kit had lost interest. He asked if he could nick my toastie crusts, one of them already half-way to his mouth.

✦

It was Sunday evening at Lenny's place. Shaz, Maeve, and I were there, and so was Jo, Lenny's sister, who was visiting from the country with her five-year-old,

Finn. Jo brought out an apple tart she'd made and took orders for hot drinks. I helped her in the kitchen, setting out milk and sugar on a tray.

'Here's Finn,' I said merrily, as he followed us in.

'Here's me,' agreed Finn, climbing onto a chair and picking up the knife his mother had used to slice the tart.

'Don't play with the knife, Finn,' said Jo, lighting the gas under the kettle, while I opened a cupboard and made a selection from Lenny's vast collection of mismatched mugs.

'Be careful with that knife, Finn,' said Jo, as we doled out tea bags and Maxwell House. 'Please put it down.'

The water boiled, I filled mugs, and, as Jo picked up the tray, Finn cut his thumb. His face crumpled, and he roared, 'Mum! You're not looking after me! *Mum!*'

◆

A week had passed and Kit hadn't called or come around.

I called him. No one answered.

I kept going back over the last time I'd seen him. He'd been more tender than usual. In retrospect it seemed ominous, the tenderness that attends farewells.

I called at various hours, including very late.

Two more days passed.

✦

'Be the one to break up. Be the one. Be the cool one.'

✦

'Who will write the history of tears?'

✦

Lying in bed, I was back in a harbourside park, looking up at a smoky green tree. 'Remember this, learn from this.' But I hadn't remembered, I hadn't learned.

✦

It was my birthday. I was twenty-five. Greetings came from Sydney friends. My mother sent twenty dollars in a card with 'For A Special Daughter' printed on the front. Inside, she wrote, 'May the bluebird of happiness fly your way.'

I went around to Anti's for gin. She didn't know that it was my birthday but she had a present for me anyway, a bottle-green tube skirt. The fabric was from Victoria Market and came in a tube, she explained. 'I bought a length of it, sewed a hem at one end, and ran some elastic through the other for a waistband. Easy as.'

I wore my tube skirt every day, with a warm, man-size black jumper. If you looked closely, you saw minute blue and red flecks in the yarn. The jumper had a tiny hole near the hem and had belonged to Reza. The sleeves extended over my fingers, and I fondled them for comfort. Annie Lennox warned that love, love, love was a dangerous drug. I listened to my neighbours listening to music, slamming doors, running their taps.

✦

Two apples had gone soft in the kitchen. I couldn't bring myself to throw them out.

✦

The bike was my hostage. I was waiting for Kit to ransom it.

I was waiting for him to want me again.

I'd be as patient as dust.

✦

At the start of winter, when my days were salty with happiness, I'd sent him away. Why?

✦

I tracked down Paula's revenge review of her rival's book. It began with a show of objectivity, offering a brief overview of recent developments in women's fiction, summarising the plot of the novel, and praising the writer for focusing on contemporary Australian life. Then it went berserk. The novel was a short one, but the review occupied a broadsheet page. It attacked the structure the novelist had devised, her treatment of temporality, her understanding of character, her handling of pace. It hewed into grammar, syntax, narrative, and style. It lashed the writer's portrayal of female unhappiness over a heterosexual relationship. That was retrograde. It was abject. It was unfeminist. Had the writer no shame? And so on and so on and so on, Paula, in the grip of her morbid symptoms, striking blow after bloody blow.

✦

There came an evening when I couldn't stop roving around my flat. In the corner of my eye, my open typewriter was a tiny piano. It was a question of keeping my balance, but it wasn't a flat that could be roved. The futon and the wardrobe, jammed in at opposite ends of the bedroom, left only a heater-wide passage between the two. As for the lounge room, I had to pick my way through the books and photocopies that obscured the carpet's revolting expanse.

A moon as red as surgical waste stood over the bay. Anti's flat was in darkness, so I rang Lenny's bell. Lenny looked at me out of his angry face, and nothing had to be explained. He asked if I fancied an Irish coffee or a brandy Alexander. I said, 'Why not both?'

With our drinks beside us, Lenny carried on marking essays. Sometimes he emitted a bark-laugh and once he muttered, 'Hoo-bloody-ray!' I borrowed a creased-spine John Berger paperback and lay on the dispirited couch. One of the lovely things about Lenny's place was the heater built into the fireplace that velveted the room with warmth. A pencil sketch I hadn't seen before was propped on the mantelpiece. It showed part of a bed, and the sleeve of a hospital gown rolled up above an arm. Taped to the wall above it was a Pissarro print of peasants working in a field. Lenny was writing a book about him. Once he'd told me, 'Pissarro was the only Impressionist in whose work domestic servants are central figures. He respected labour – all those tiny dabs of paint.'

✦

I spotted Olivia among a group of students near the Philosophy building. Her painterly hair hung loose, and the wind was whipping it across her face. She wiped it away as I watched, and tucked it behind her ear.

'There's no need to bring her into this' – but Olivia was *always already* there. Sometimes I fell asleep thinking about her and woke thinking about her the next day. Sometimes I remembered with incredulity that, just a few months before, I'd hardly thought of her at all. It encouraged me to believe that I could easily return to that state – it would require no more effort than opening a window or changing my shoes. But every day, under every aspect of my life, Olivia ran like a stream. In this world only one of us two could be happy, I thought. Why shouldn't the bluebird of happiness fly my way?

The group around Olivia was about to break up – one of the others was turning away. It felt imperative to display myself to Olivia. I was wearing my green tube skirt, and before stepping forward I unbuttoned my jacket to reveal my Madonna-style ropes of plastic pearls. I was acting robotically, powered by an emotion as undiluted and primitive as the hunger that had driven me to claw at Kit. Paula's lethal review was a public execution, but it was also a scream of defeat. Each wound she inflicted on her rival was a confession of rejection and suffering. I vowed never to give Olivia the satisfaction of knowing I cared that Kit had chosen her over me. Smiling at her in a cordial yet inattentive way, I passed without pausing to register her reaction. *I am busy, I am stylish, I am indifferent to you: behold!*

✦

That evening I asked Anti if she ever had negative thoughts about other women. 'Negative' was a late swap. I'd been heading for 'hateful' at first.

'Baby, is it possible I haven't told you about Nadine? Ed's ex. Their circles overlap, and that's the first problem – there's no escaping her. They split up two years ago, and she found a new guy pretty much at once, you should see him, urrgh, his head is a basketball, but she has a little special smile, a twinkly look in her eyes, that she saves for Ed. She always remembers his birthday. He thinks it's sweet. Men! How the fuck did they get to run everything when they haven't got a brain among them? Nadine *will not* keep her distance, which is the only decent way to behave with your ex. Someone will mention, I don't know, Italy, and she'll put her hand on Ed's arm, and look up at him with her special smile, and say, "Remember our waiter in Urbino?" And then she'll tell some *hilarious*, frankly racist story that illustrates what she calls "the Mediterranean mindset". She's got this collection of cashmere cardigans. I dream of strangling her with the sleeves.'

Anti went on to say that in her father's village in Greece, the villagers had a traditional method of placing a curse on an enemy: they'd write the enemy's name on a slip of paper and place it in a freezer so that ice formed over it. 'Maybe in the old days people used to wait for winter and bury the paper under snow, but us wogs are adaptive. We've modernised.'

'Does the enemy die?' I asked, Thrilled to the Marrow. 'Are you testing it on Nadine?'

Anti pulled an ambiguous face.

✦

'Harvey has been suspended from school for drugs. He and some other boys were caught smoking marijuana and it is lucky the Police were not called in. This is the child Babs puts on her head and walks. When I think of all the rubbish she talks about how Catholic schools are better than State schools. She took care not to say a word about Harvey, of course, but Colin let the cat out of the bag. Babs was wild! She would have given him hell after they dropped me off. I pray for you every day, for you to pass your degree with flying colours. I am enclosing a nice recipe for Stuffed Tomatoes that I got from a vegetarian girl at work.'

✦

I'd started riding with cautious nonchalance along the calm residential streets behind my building. One morning a terrier barrelled out of a gate and nipped my calf through my leggings. His owner flew out after him, dragged him into her yard, and shut the gate. She apologised and apologised, and said he was a gentle soul, really, but the sound of a bicycle chain sent him into a frenzy. She said it was her fault, really, for not making sure the gate was shut, and she wanted to drive me to a doctor. Inside the house, a baby started to wail. Inspecting my leg, I said I was all right, really, the bite had barely broken my skin. The woman made me promise to get a tetanus shot, and asked for my phone number and address. She really needed to check that I was okay, she said.

◆

The ring-a-roses on my leg, oozing a little blood, brought me to my senses. The terrier, a sensible beast, had tried to get rid of what he couldn't bear. As long as that bike was around, I couldn't free myself of Kit. If I couldn't free myself of Kit, I couldn't free myself of Olivia. On top of that, I was fed up with the vicious kicks my hostage delighted in landing on my shins.

That evening I hefted it down the stairs and walked it over to Kit's. Clouds were heading the same way, as purposeful as trams. Kit's flat was upstairs at the back of the block. Two windows glowed there, and I cast a few glances at them, but I had no way of working out if they were his.

The 'garage' was only a ramshackle three-sided shed. I propped the bike in the rack at one end, padlocked it, and dropped the key in Kit's letterbox. In the street, swollen with bravado, I almost crashed into Maeve. She held up a foil takeaway bag and said she was on her way to a friend's place with a roast chook.

I was steps away from my gate when the terrier's owner came out of the dark with an armful of flames. 'With sincere apologies from Diggy,' said the card with the flowers. Diggy's orange tulips burned against my grubby grey walls, filling three glasses and a jug. I woke that night, saw light squeezed into petals and believed I could smell it. I dialled Olivia's number and hung up. I was about to call Kit, but remembered him turning up at my flat on that long-ago Sunday in a gust of mud-scented air. If I heard his voice now, I'd come unstuck.

✦

I celebrated the arrival of spring by coming down with flu. Lenny brought me soup and mandarins, but all I could eat was unbuttered toast. I staggered between my futon and the bathroom or the kitchen. My eyes were tightly hot, and every other part of me was icy. Sleeping, I wound and unwound my bedclothes, trying to keep warm, trying to get cool. For a peaceful half-hour, I floated above my bed like a Chagall bride.

My mother called. She said I sounded hoarse, so I told her I'd been teaching and had strained my voice. I didn't say I was ill, because what kind of mother needlessly causes her daughter distress?

She asked, 'How long before Christmas are you coming home?'

'It's September! I haven't a clue what I'll be doing in three months.' It was all too easy to picture her in her flat, where every surface was furred with loneliness and obsessively clean. Walking into the sadness and dimness and clutter of that flat was like walking into my mother's mind. Being entirely capable of a little torture even – or especially – when weak, I added, 'I might not be able to come back for Christmas. I'll have to see.'

Afterwards I lay in bed longing for a bowl of boiled white rice swimming in Vegemite soup, which was Vegemite dissolved in hot water, a dish devised by my mother and the only food I craved when ill.

✦

Late that night the phone rang. It stopped before I could summon the strength to lift the receiver. I lay there hoping the caller was Olivia. But if it was, where was Kit? I wanted to call him but I fell asleep.

At dawn the kind mirror revealed a mahogany-coloured wretch and a sea of mucusy tissues. The tulips had fainted and dropped their petals. Their stalks persisted in waterless containers, anaemic memorials to silk and blaze. I ran out of Kleenex and fell back on toilet paper. I missed the opening of Anti's show.

◆

My mother was evicted from her flat and moved in with me. It made me cough myself awake. What was extra horrible about the dream was that my flat, like hers, was over-furnished and overlooked a busy road – in fact it *was* her flat. I couldn't get back to sleep for a long time. The past was brightly lit and full of danger. Old things crawled about in my chest.

I realised, with the clarity of illness, that my impression of unreality at that birthday party in Glebe had nothing to do with estrangement from my surroundings as I'd previously thought. I wasn't estranged from those surroundings at all. They belonged to the classy world at which I was aiming, the world for which my university was fitting me, the world for which we'd migrated to Australia. My real estrangement was from the world I'd left behind. I had the measure of my distance from it that evening: seven kilometres, the distance to my parents' flat.

Their flat was the antithesis of the tall, pleasant house, where I'd made light, pleasant conversation with rich, pleasant people. My first, worst years in Australia had been spent in that flat, where my mother still lived. I kept trying to persuade her to move into a one-bedder, which would be cheaper and free of painful associations, but she always refused. I could tell that a fantastic Technicolor film, in which I returned to my old bedroom to live with her forever, screened perpetually in a fold of her brain. Every inch of her flat was intimately familiar to me, but for a long time now, I'd been unable to contemplate it without feeling squeamish. The name for that entwined closeness and distance was weirdness. The Death of the Father was a given, but what about *always already* Undead Mother, clutching at her lively daughters from the grave?

✦

'Do you have any throat lozenges like Strepsils? I'm so worried about you. Teaching must put a terrible strain on your voice. I can send lozenges from here if they are not easily obtainable in Melbourne or expensive. I can send <u>anything</u> you need, even money.'

✦

Anti came by in a leather cap, bearing strawberries and cream. We sat out on my rickety back stairs to eat them, looking spring in the face. It was a mild, sunny afternoon, and strength was stirring in me like light. The creeper across the street had put out disciplined leaves in elemental green. I hoped that the sun would find its way into the cold, dark corners of my mind. Anti took off her shoes and socks, and I did the same. We flexed our toes and dipped our spoons in our bowls. I didn't tell Anti that I missed the hullaballoo of Sydney in spring. I missed the irreverence of birds who addressed each other with cymbals, and the bougainvilleas' unbridled ejaculations. Spring here was like the people, polished and knowing exactly what to wear.

In any case, Anti had no interest in the mannerly display around us. The *Age* art critic had panned her show. Waving her creamy spoon, she recited his summing up: '"These works, tensely Eurocentric even to their monochrome palette, have little to say to Australia." My mother's part Italian, my father's part Romanian, we're fully wogs, the junta murdered half my relatives. So this dickhead, what's he expect? Blue sky, red earth, kookaburra shitting in the old gum tree? Ed says he wants a multiculti cartoon: fluffy dice in muscle cars and widows in black hosing down concrete and hairy men smashing plates.'

✦

A corner of the screen door in my kitchen had come away from its frame. Tiny new flies revolved gently in my flat. They were as persistent as the fishbone ferns pushing up against the fence when I carried my rubbish down to the bins. Spring! I peered into the ice cave of my freezer compartment: time to defrost! The following afternoon I started transferring long slabs of ice from the fridge to the sink.

Two small index cards lay on my desk. One listed names for the daughter I'd never have with Kit. Not Jean. Not Virginia. *Not my name.* I couldn't decide whether to carry out my plan for the other card. Weakened by flu, I was subject to many morbid symptoms. My hands felt frozen after a while, and scraping at stubborn ice with a flat-bladed knife exhausted me. I went back to bed and read for the rest of the day.

✦

At the end of Tolstoy's novella *The Death of Ivan Ilyich*, someone watching over the dying man sees that the end is imminent and says, 'It is finished.'

Ivan Ilyich, misunderstanding this, believes that death is finished. 'It is no more,' he thinks. He takes a breath and dies.

At the start of winter I'd told Kit that we were finished. Later, I'd let myself believe that we were not. I'd been as contented as Ivan Ilyich, and as wrong.

✦

The underlying smells in my flat were three: cold ashes, blow heater, typewriter ribbon. I was working on my seminar paper again. I was thinking about Woolves. Of course Leonard minded when his wife called him 'the Jew' or 'my Jew'. Of course he didn't show that he did. That was the meaning of assimilation: it trained us not to show that we minded. It trained us to pass. It trained us to disappear.

What would Leonard have got if he'd shown that he minded?

No election to the exclusive Cambridge Apostles.

No Thoby and Adrian Stephen, brothers to Virginia.

No Bloomsbury.

No brilliant, beautiful, mentally ill, impeccably connected, upper-middle-class Gentile wife.

No Distinction.

No Pass With Merit.

No Pass.

What did my mother get when she chose heartfelt, unassimilated colours that added lustre to her face? A daughter who bared her wolfish, assimilated teeth.

Why is your makeup so obvious?

Why won't you wear navy?

What's wrong with beige?

When will you stop dyeing your hair?

Why won't you wear cobwebs?
Dirt is a tasteful colour.
Cement is a neutral.
What's *wrong* with you?
Why won't you disappear?

✦

A fresh fantasy grew all-consuming. Olivia left our table at Leo's, and, as soon as she'd entered the ladies, I shifted her bag onto my lap. First there was the blind handling of objects within it, the feeling-out of shapes. Then I stole a pocket diary/money/lip balm/a vial of perfume/a pen. The clasp on the chain that held Olivia's golden heart had broken, and she'd stored it in her bag to keep it safe. I unzipped the inside pocket and helped myself, dribbling the cold links through my fingers. At night, I'd lie in bed and reward myself with looping replays of the scene. It got to the point where I forgot that Olivia hadn't left the table, and reproached myself for not having had the presence of mind to carry out the thefts.

✦

On an October morning when the wind was bullying blossoms, Mrs Walker's windows were bare. Her orange curtains lay bundled on a heap of newspapers, one of many in the yard. A tanned, handsome man in a boiler suit came out of the boarding house with his arms full of flattened cardboard, treading so determinedly that he seemed to part the air.

Further along the street, workers were tearing up the pavement and there was a terrible stench. I went back to the boarding house and asked the man if Mrs Walker had moved out.

He ran his hand through his bouncy hair. 'You a friend?'

'Neighbour.'

'I'm the landlord here. Look at all this junk!' His Blundstone nudged the nearest pile of papers. 'Fire hazard. She had plenty of warning.'

'Where's she gone?'

'Tell me when you find out. I've rent owing.' His eyes wandered, as if he were trying to pin down a large, difficult truth. Then his shoulders sagged. 'Pearl Walker's gone walkabout, love. Shot through with my money. End of story.'

He spoke as if there was only one story about possession and theft. My mind went to the poster on Lenny's door that featured a Black woman on a beach. Against the different blues of sea and sky, she faced outwards with her hands on her hips. Her gaze, her stance, and the colours were assertive. The caption told The Story Under All The Stories of Australia: 'YOU ARE ON ABORIGINAL LAND.'

✦

In the early stages of planning *The Years*, when Woolf was thinking about what she wanted to achieve with her new book, she wrote, 'I will go on adventuring, changing, opening my mind & my eyes, refusing to be stamped & stereotyped.' I'd copied her declaration onto an index card and presented it to Anti in the aftermath of her show. Anti spray-painted the quote onto a length of fabric, and I went to her studio to help her string it up across a wall. 'Ten minutes with her and I'd be calling for a gun,' said Anti dreamily, contemplating her banner. 'But she helped build my brain. You know?'

✦

The phone rang late at night. 'Kit,' I said. 'Kit.'

My caller hung up.

All through that spring, branches rapped in the wind, and my windows rapped in their frames. I'd startle awake to rapping, thinking Kit was at my door. But it was only the wind.

✦

Lenny and Shaz were coming to dinner, but Lenny called that afternoon to cancel. 'Lost another mate.

Robbie, Daz, Ari, Peter, Kurt, Mike, Craig, that's just this year. Aiden today. He was twenty-two.'

✦

Sometimes jealousy was a visitor from an alien galaxy that had nothing to do with me. Sometimes it was a frightening growth in my body for which science hadn't discovered a cure.

Shortly after coming across the letter from Lois I'd stood in a bookshop reading *A Lover's Discourse*. It was expensive, but I bought it at once. Yes, yes, yes, I muttered orgasmically to myself as I read, yes, that's it exactly. Barthes' lover knew what it was like to be me. He desired and was foolish and waited and despaired. He was jealous. He recognised the complexity of jealousy. He obliged himself to accept non-exclusive relationships and wondered whether doing so was really an inverted conformism: 'because I was ashamed to be jealous'. I wanted to re-read that passage now, but my dog-eared copy had disappeared. I searched my flat before concluding that Kit must have stolen the book and ripped out the flyleaf with my name.

Perhaps Olivia was lying in Kit's bed reading it at this moment, silently muttering, Yes, yes, yes. She'd realise that her acquiescence in their deconstructed relationship had its origin in shame. She'd be struck, as I'd been, by the tremendous silencing power of shame. To whom could we confess our treacherous, rivalrous, trite, uncool, unfeminist feelings without shame? Shame could transform female solidarity into a scold's bridle. It could ensure that a philosophy designed to free us set a weight on our tongues.

✦

'And I got one of the scholarships, but because I didn't get the highest mark, Mum said it was "a disappointing result".'

We howled like wolves at Shaz's story. 'That sounds exactly like my mum!' we cried, and 'Honestly, the stuff they come up with!' and 'Hope my kids shoot me if I end up like that!'

Shaz was celebrating her birthday with a women-only lunch. Obviously the occasion called for mauling our mothers, tearing into them with our pointy teeth. As daughters, it was our duty and our fate to disappoint them, we agreed, and we swore we'd go on doing so. We howled and howled, and tears ran down our cheeks.

Etsuko played keyboards in Says Ann. She was ripping up and howling too, but then she broke off. She asked, 'Does anyone want to end up like her father instead?'

✦

My buzzer went. Kit's voice said, 'Can I have my dish back?'

'What?'

I'd forgotten about it, truly.

'My lasagne dish.'

'You gave me that dish.'

'I need it.'

He sounded unhappy.

A truck changed gear in the street.

I stood on a chair and fetched his/my/his enamel dish down from its shelf. Grey with dust, it contained a disintegrating fly.

When I'd placed the dish on the landing and shut my door, I spoke into the answerphone and pressed the button that opened the door to the street.

In the bathroom I inserted a fresh tampon. I washed my hands and dried them on a towel where I'd once found bright brown hairs. We'd studied in my cast-iron, claw-footed bath, studied in the shower with its curved, pressed-metal, art deco surround. The tampon I'd had inside me now lay warmly, crimsonly swollen alongside the fly in the grimy dish. My period had never deterred us, flowering Kit's penis, blossoming my sheets. Let Olivia eat lasagne spiced with blood and death. Let every one of them, Mops and Pobby and Amabel and Kit, taste my loving gifts.

✦

'Who will write the history of tears?'

✦

The index card I slipped into Kit's letterbox relayed the monster's promise to Dr Frankenstein: 'I will be with you on your wedding night.'

✦

The paper that I read to the postgraduates was called 'Virginia Woolf's Tea'. I began with the importance of afternoon tea in Victorian Britain, and moved on to Woolf's rejection of the ceremony as symbolising her rejection of outmoded female roles. Afternoon tea diminishes in status in *The Years* as Woolf's female characters move towards emancipation, I said. When Rose, a suffragette, thinks of her childhood, she can feel nostalgia for the elaborate ritual because it no longer has power over her life.

I pointed out that the fortunes of the Pargiters are bound up with empire. The men in the family come and go from imperial outposts as soldiers or landowners; the patriarch has lost two fingers in what was known, in Woolf's day, as the Indian Mutiny. Towards the end of the novel, an Indian guest in a pink turban appears at a party given in London by Delia Pargiter. Described as 'one of Eleanor's Indians', he serves to signify progressive values in the Pargiter set. Woolf tells us that Delia and Eleanor talk to him, but she gives him nothing to say.

I touched on the role played by tea in the history of the empire. After the Opium Wars in China, tea began to be cultivated in British colonies. The labour force on the tea estates was made up of indentured workers, cajoled or coerced away from their ancestral lands. The indenture system, instituted after the abolition of slavery, ensured that the lives of plantation workers were played out in abysmal conditions. They lived in squalid, crowded quarters without running water or adequate sanitation, and received no medical care. The men were employed in the factories that processed the tea leaves, while the women laboured as pluckers, their small hands better suited to that delicate task. No schooling was provided for their children, who would eventually replace their parents on the estates.

I contrasted the modernising trajectory of Woolf's Englishwomen and the ongoing immiseration of the tea pluckers. The former was made possible by the latter, by the exploitative colonial practices that underwrote British progress and wealth. I told my audience that Woolf had set out to find a fresh form in *The Years*, but had later abandoned the attempt. A fresh form represents a desire to see the world differently, but Woolf hadn't managed to do so. *The Years* remained enclosed in the powerful fiction that the self-fulfilment of British women transcended the imperialism that enabled it. That was The Story Under The Story in *The Years*. Like the Indian at the party, it was a narrative presence denied a voice.

The 'discovery' that concluded my paper was exactly what I'd set out to find. It was one of many notes I struck to produce the authorised discursive music, interrogating, positing, foregrounding, summoning a cold-eyed assistant called the Suspicious Reader and exhibiting my mastery over the text. The pink-turbaned Indian was my final, resounding chord: the minor figure who turned out to hold the key to the hidden meaning of *The Years*.

I hadn't invited Paula to the seminar. But she was there anyway, her face set to Encouraging and placed where I couldn't avoid seeing it. In questions, she began by praising my reading as 'wonderfully suggestive'. She added that the interpretative possibilities of *The Years* could never be exhausted since no text has settled signifieds. She flashed her bloody teeth and asked a question I couldn't answer involving an essay by a feminist theorist whom I hadn't read.

Afterwards I ran away with Elise and a few other postgrads to Johnny's Green Room, where we ate spaghetti marinara made with tinned sardines and drank too much carafe wine. When I got home I had to set the Woolfmother straight. I couldn't do otherwise, I explained, as I Blu Tacked her unstuck corners into place. A daughter was obliged to point out her mother's shortcomings; it couldn't be helped. Had she expected applause for granting an Indian entry into an English drawing room on condition that he didn't speak? The Woolfmother continued to avoid my eye, her creative-destructive energies fizzing, my boot print half obscuring her face.

✦

'If I have a fall I suppose you will find me lying dead on the floor.'

✦

We were gathering at Lenny's for pizza one evening, when Benedict arrived and told us that a stranger had spat at him in Safeway. 'She said I was touching everything and spreading my filthy disease. She had this little kid with her, and she shoved him behind her like he needed protecting from me.' Benedict had left without his groceries. 'I don't think I can go back there again.'

Lenny started talking about the need for information and how the government wasn't doing anywhere near enough to educate people. Shaz cut him off. 'Yeah, I'm sure that's all necessary, mate, but you know what I want to do? I want to scream. I want to scream and scream at all the stupidity and hatred and death, and I'm going out to do it right now.' She was on her feet, reaching for her parka. 'Coming?'

That's how I remember us: screaming as we stride along the Esplanade, Shaz out in front in her silver parka, Benedict's year-round thongs slapping beside Lenny's sneakers, Maeve's fist pumping, the trailing banner of Anti's orange scarf. We scream past the square with its war memorial; we scream past the glaring ocean liner of the pub. We scream our way across Marine Parade and, when we reach the pier, we break into a run. We pound along screaming as if to fling ourselves into the bay. We still have our young, unprepared faces. The sodium lights curving overhead have their mouths as wide as ours, setting a runny yellow glow on the water. Beyond their reach, the darkness mumbles and shrugs.

✦

I strolled down the pied-à-terre street, walked around the block, and strolled along the pied-à-terre street again. Then I strolled past Mops's gallery. It had clerestory windows, so I couldn't see inside. A poster on the door advertised the current show with a savagely repellent image in oranges and pinks.

It was Friday afternoon. In Brunswick Street I bought a savagely repellent orangey-pink lipstick in a gold case, went into the post office, and sent it to my mother, who would love it on sight. Before posting it I scraped off most of the price sticker but left the first digit after the dollar sign. My mother would see that I'd paid more than twenty dollars, a sum that represented Unimaginable Extravagance to her. She'd save the lipstick for a special occasion that would never arrive, and every time she opened a drawer and saw it, her happiness at such overwhelming proof of my love would be complicated by her terror at my spendthrift ways.

A notice in the window of a newish cafe caught my eye. It announced that the violin duo Orpheus would be performing on the following Sunday at 3 pm. The musicians' names were given underneath. I wondered if Kit would be there on Sunday to hear Amabel and Olivia, and whether Mops and Pobby would show up as well. My mind foamed with envy and loathing of parents who conversed in cafes about music and art. The envy spilled over and encompassed Olivia's past. I imagined her growing up in Mount Macedon in an atmosphere of easy-going creativity and open-mindedness, with lively dinner-table conversations where no subject was forbidden, and adults who accepted childish transgressions and forgave them at once.

✦

My parents had grown up in households where music meant the radio. Neither of them had learned to play an instrument. My father's family was cheerfully unmusical, my mother's merely poor. She was the one who insisted that I have music lessons. At the end, when my piano was carried out of our house, she remarked with sad resignation on its absence. Our rooms now consisted of nothing but spaces where furniture had stood, but my mother's gaze was pulled to the spot where there was no longer a piano. I found it vaguely irritating, too young to grasp that the loss she was mourning was distance climbed.

In Sydney my parents acquired a record player and records by singers like Frank Sinatra and Neil Diamond and Johnny Cash. I realised that I hadn't seen the player or the records in a while. When my mother rang to thank me for the lipstick, I asked if she still listened to music. She often had the radio on, she said. I mentioned the records, and she told me she'd donated them and the player to a church for its Christmas fair. I pushed and pressed, and finally she said that those records made her 'feel bad'.

In my mother's idiom, 'feeling bad' covered the spectrum from fleeting disappointment to suicidal ideation. The phone call ended, and I lay in bed feeling bad that:

I was the kind of daughter who let the price sticker show on the savagely repellent lipstick I bought for my widowed mother;

She was the kind of mother who didn't find the lipstick savagely repellent;

Neither of us could break out of a situation I found savagely repellent and to which I was sadly resigned.

✦

Day after November day, pollen from privet and freshly leaved plane trees brought on my hay fever. Antihistamines felled me, so I chose itchy eyes and blowing my nose raw. Language-lab classes had ended for the year, I'd marked my students' final tests and now I was concentrating on my thesis. I worked at home because my tremendous sneezes annoyed the students studying for exams in the library. The mahogany-coloured wretch was no longer showing up, so I assumed that my paper had appeased him. I was free to posit and demystify and interrogate, and was doing so with suspicious ease.

On a blustery afternoon I found mail in my letterbox. Identical envelopes protruded from my neighbours' boxes, too. The sheet of paper inside bore a real estate agency's letterhead, but it was really a letter from Late Capitalism. In January my rent would be going up to two hundred and thirty dollars a month, an increase of twenty-five per cent.

✦

The sunset was a murderous red stripe over the bay. Little waves went on sounding their note of baffled rage.

✦

Anti took me to a school fete where she foraged every year. It was a school for the sons of the wealthy, and I was astounded by what the rich didn't want. We sorted through rails of designer clothing and samples, electrical goods donated because they weren't the latest model, racks of barely worn shoes. I bought books and leggings for myself, and an outrageously flowered blouse for my mother. Anti scooped up a kitchen blender, and a variety of jetsam to use in installations. Then she pounced on a pair of spike-heeled golden sandals, saucer-size golden earrings, and a sweeping, off-the-shoulder magenta dress. 'Family wedding coming up. I'm going the whole wog.'

Afterwards, on our way up to her place, we ran into Lenny coming down the stairs. Proud as pirates, we displayed our loot and urged him to join us in a drink. But he was on his way to meet Olivia and Kit. A mining company had offered Kit a job in Western Australia, he told us, and Olivia had organised an impromptu celebration in Fitzroy.

Anti said, 'Isn't Kit still at uni?'

'Almost through.' Olivia's father was on the board

of the company, Lenny explained. 'They're taking Kit on at the end of summer. Conditional on getting through his exams, but Kit's pretty sure he'll be right.'

He went on his way. Anti and I went up to her balcony. '"Kit's pretty sure he'll be right",' quoted Anti, unscrewing the cap on the gin. 'Yeah, I'm pretty sure he'll be right, too. Why is that? Could it be because Anglo Daddy's sorted his future?'

When I was an undergraduate I'd worked out exactly how much I could drink to loosen up and still feel in control. For the past three Saturday nights, I'd been taking myself to hear bands in pubs. The man whose drinks I accepted and followed into a lane on the first Saturday had something of Kit's tight-skinned look around the jaw. On the following Saturday I kissed a man all the way down the graffitied corridor leading to the ladies, where we entered a cubicle and locked the door. The third Saturday was drizzly, and the air felt extravagantly soft. In a deserted residential street, the smell of earth and greenery was strong. The man I'd danced with all evening picked the lock on a Holden – every Australian was born knowing how to do it, he said, as we lay down on the seat.

Anti had it wrong, I told her: it was Olivia's future that Anglo Daddy had sorted. A pied-à-terre or a husband, either made a thoughtful gift. The bay had the look of a mouthful of fillings. 'Anyway, who cares about those people?' I said, keeping my gaze on that steely gape.

✦

'A girl called Judy Carstairs who recently bought number 43 asked me to feed her cats while she is in Brisbane for work (she is a lady Lawyer). The cats are beautiful specimens called Fluffy and Brass. Brass has to be fed on the kitchen bench and Fluffy will only eat from a red plate! Judy phoned yesterday to find out how they are. Just think, she is only twenty-nine and already owns her own house. She must be earning very well. You'll remember that your father and I advised you to study Law. After giving the cats their dinner, I sit with them for quite a long time. Brass likes to curl up on my lap. I told Judy that I would miss them when she comes back, and she asked why I don't get a cat. What is the use, you get attached and then they have to be put down.'

✦

A noise between a bellow and a howl was going on and on, suggesting an animal in mortal pain. I went downstairs to the Friday night razzamatazz of crowds, neon, car stereos, gridlock. A man was hauling himself and his bags of possessions along the far side of the street, halting now and then. His wordless protest rose and fell. For a week or so I heard it every evening around eight. Then it never came again.

✦

Olivia and Kit were sure to be at the party for Lenny's thirtieth, so I got changed three times and redid my makeup twice. I put on a bra and took it off again. Finally, with my bed covered in discarded clothing, I settled on a lilac petticoat with lace at the V of the bodice and on the straps. My hair had grown enough to be piled up loosely, and the diamante clasp on my glittery choker was missing several stones. Look out, world, I told my reflection, here comes Slutty! On the way out, I stopped and went back to the kind mirror. I took the plastic combs from my hair and gave it a shake so that it fell around my face.

With the coming of summer, Melbourne had turned into Sydney. Deafening sunlight had arrived, and thick, moist air. The Galleon had started to serve iced coffee, 'Colder Than Your Ex's Heart'. But when the bay came into view as I headed to Lenny's, cumulus mountains were arranged along the horizon. The evening felt jumpy, spoiling for a fight.

Lenny's balcony was packed. People were also sitting on the stairs near the landing window, hoping for a breeze. I saw the back of Olivia's golden head as I passed through the lounge on my way to the kitchen. Heaps of people had brought food. I shifted bowls and platters, clearing a space on the table for my asparagus quiche.

Maeve, ravishing in faded cotton, asked if I wanted to serve the quiche warm. She had a pasta bake in the fridge that she intended to heat up later, and she could do my quiche at the same time. I said that room temperature would be fine. Maeve was frowning – she was worried that a pasta bake was wrong for the weather. 'But it's the one thing I know how to cook. And it's best served warm, with the cheese all melty.'

I loved a pasta bake at any time of year, I assured her, slicing up the quiche. Maeve said she had so much to get through in the next few days, she couldn't think straight. She was moving out of her share house, off to Darwin and then on to Indonesia. She'd be spending the summer there, studying traditional dance. She passed me a bottle. I filled Lenny's largest mug with champagne.

In the lounge, Amabel called, 'There you are,' shouldering her way towards me. 'Liv and I were just wondering when you'd get here.' I muttered something about deciding at the last minute to have a cold shower, it was so hot, and Amabel said it was fascinating that I still had a Sydney accent. 'You're probably stuck with it for good.'

'What's a Sydney accent?' someone asked.

'Shau-WAH. Sum-MAH.'

I drank champagne.

There was singing on the balcony. Benedict, heading for the door, said he'd run out of cigarettes. 'Want anything from the shop?'

He left, and the wind arrived. The bathroom door slammed shut. The singing grew louder, and I recognised Shaz's grainy voice: 'Remember what Adorno said / Feed your head.' The song soon collapsed in laughter, rowdiness. People started moving into the lounge room. Shaz barged over to me, grinning, with a stubbie. 'Hey, look at you, ya big spunk! Now all we need is Anti.'

'Didn't Lenny say? It's her cousin's wedding. She can't come.'

Kit had followed Shaz inside. I watched him see me and decide not to. I could still summon the smell of his skin, cold and sweet like alcohol. He went over to the crowd around Lenny, and helped himself from a spread of snacks.

Thunder crashed.

The rain came.

Voices rose, the room darkened, things turned elemental.

Benedict helter-skeltered through the front door, his pale hair, blackened by rain, plastered to his skull.

My dress felt glutinous against my skin. I grabbed a chunk of cheese and some crackers from a platter, and ate them peering out from the balcony door. The bay had disappeared behind an aluminium veil. Rain running off the roof was blowing in onto the balcony, where puddles were forming on the tiles. Somewhere close at hand, a baby was crying. A man wearing only shorts came running down the street, clutching a plastic bag over his head. Cars swooshed past like swords.

The Mac was in its usual place on Lenny's desk, only now it was set with twirly pink candles, covered in coffee icing and made of cake. The screen said HAPPY BIRTHDAY in chocolate Times New Roman, and the keyboard spelled ALL DOWNHILL NOW. This marvel was Anti's creation. I gave Lenny his present, a collection of poems by Elizabeth Bishop. Over his shoulder, I caught and held Kit's eye. We nodded at each other, and then we both looked away. I made a great performance of admiring the cake.

Olivia was squeezing her way over. 'You look lovely,' she said, and kissed me. 'Isn't it hot!' She fanned herself with her hand. She was wearing a light cotton dress with balloon sleeves gathered at the wrist. The green-and-white Indian blockprint, dabbed here and there with gold, brought lilies to mind. I saw myself slipping into her bedroom, yanking the dress off its hanger, ripping it apart. In spite of what she'd said, Olivia looked cool and virginal, like a lily. She touched her expensive heart.

Because silence between us was unbearable, I said the first thing that came into my head. 'Did Simone de Beauvoir ever write back to you?'

Olivia looked surprised. 'I didn't expect her to. It was writing the letter that mattered.'

I shifted my weight onto the other foot. I wished I'd thought of writing to de Beauvoir.

Shaz, offering us a plate of julienned vegetables and baba ghanoush, asked Olivia if her jewellery ghost was still around.

'Oh, you remembered that. I feel so silly.' Spring-cleaning her room, Olivia had moved a chest away from the wall. There lay her missing jewellery. 'I keep clothes on top of that chest between washes. Sometimes when I was rushing and grabbed something to wear, I must have sent a piece of jewellery into the gap behind the chest.'

The packed room obliged us to stand uncomfortably close. Olivia was sipping champagne – not from a tumbler or a mug or a plastic cup like everyone else, but from a flute. For all I knew she'd brought it with her. The clear golden liquid seemed to gather and hold all the light in the room.

Kit had moved closer and was talking to Shaz. He was wearing a loose, paisley shirt that looked new. Amabel was there, too – Amabel was always there – with a fistful of chips. 'It's so colonial to rely on people speaking English,' I heard her say. She turned to me, yanking me into the conversation: 'You're a languages person – tell him. Tell him to take a phrasebook with him at least.'

At once I thought, He's going to Paris with Olivia. Kit was laughing at Amabel, so I managed a little laugh, too, as if she'd made a joke.

Shaz asked Kit where he was off to.

'London.'

'Kit's going to England to visit his sister,' explained Olivia. 'But he's spending some time in Bali first.' She looked at him. 'Are you still thinking of stopping off on the way back as well?'

'Hope you're not flying Garuda.' Shaz launched into a story about a flight on which an overalled mechanic armed with a tool kit jumped up from his seat and rushed towards the cockpit whenever the plane struck turbulence.

Unseen by the others, Kit raised his stubbie in my direction and took a long swig. I slid away, Thrilled to the Marrow. He was going away alone! At once, my resolutions and attitudes were of no importance. We'd meet in Paris as if we'd never been apart. On a grey boulevard, we'd eat roasted chestnuts from a newspaper cone. There was fizz in my blood, I was airborne. My mind was stringing itself along a sequence of calculations: my bank balance, the exchange rate, airfares. While this was going on, I was charming to strangers, altogether delightful. One of them, an oceanographer with a scruffy beard, touched my arm lightly as he talked. The two of us stepped away from other people, to the extent that was possible. I leaned against a shadowy wall.

The wind had turned and was charging through the room. My nipples pushed up against my dress, and I knew, from his fierce concentration on my face, that the oceanographer was thinking about them. Maybe, I thought, maybe. I arched my rib cage and smiled promises. The oceanographer said that he was very good at back massage, he had the technique down pat. At the same moment Kit lifted my dress, burrowing into me on nylon sheets.

When it was time to eat, Shaz came over to sit on the floor with us. She gave my thigh a secret, meaningful pinch when the oceanographer praised my quiche. He told us about a party he'd recently attended to celebrate the birth of his nephew. His sister-in-law was Latvian, and at the pagan-inspired naming ceremony her relatives encircled the baby singing, 'The wise man is born in the sauna.'

From the kitchen came Maeve with a tea towel over one shoulder, crying, 'Sorry, sorry, I timed this all wrong. But everyone have some of this – please.' She'd set the hot dish on a breadboard that she was bearing across the room, stepping over outstretched legs with a dancer's precise grace. Her bare feet were as clean as a baby's, with innocent pink heels. She placed the board on Lenny's desk, frowned, and said, 'I'll just grab a serving spoon.'

Hours seemed to pass, but that can't be right since Maeve was still out of the room. Some guy was already digging into her bake, plunging a cake server into the dish. The room had tightened. Objects gained outlines, receded, came close. Maeve's dish seemed to overflow the table, her white enamel dish with its blue rim. There must be heaps of dishes like that, I reasoned. The roots of my hair went cold.

Kit and Olivia had settled on the floor at an angle to me. There were people all around them, but their bodies, slightly turned to each other, made a private space. Kit put down his fork as I watched, and touched Olivia's cheek. He held out his hand to her, palm up, index finger extended. Olivia bent forward with pursed lips, closed her eyes, blew the eyelash from the tip of his finger. I wondered what she'd wished for, and whether it involved Kit, and what chance it had of coming true. Many years had to pass before I'd realise that life isn't about wishes coming true but about the slow revelation of what we really wished.

✦

Packing up my flat in the week before Christmas, I found greeny-grey mould petalling on the underside of my futon.

I found *A Lover's Discourse* under my yellow armchair.

I found a clenched white shell just like the pasta in Maeve's bake.

◆

When I returned to Melbourne after Christmas, I moved into a Richmond semi with Elise. One afternoon in April, Olivia was sitting with friends in the coffee lounge at uni. A small tremor went through me – she'd cut off her hair. Razor-short at the sides and back, it sprang upright on her crown like a sheaf of wheat. She was by a window, and the autumn sun shining on her hair made me want to touch it lightly, to feel its springy golden prickle on the pads of my fingers. I collected my coffee and went away, thinking about a paradox described in *A Lover's Discourse*: in triangular relationships, the rival, too, is loved, swelling in the lover's obsessive mind while the loved one recedes.

All the while I was squishing my ideas about Woolf's novels into the corset of Theory. It constricted and upheld my work as it was designed to do. When it was done, 'Adventuring, Changing: The Gendered Self in the Late Fiction of Virginia Woolf' was perfectly shapely and perfectly fulfilled the requirements of the university. I think of it now with a shiver of shame.

Paula took me out to lunch and urged me to go on to a doctorate. We were drinking champagne, and her lips left artery-red imprints on her glass. The tenured lectureship in the department had gone to Guy, although he'd published only in journals and Paula had a second book coming out. The academy needed feminist scholars, she told me. 'We have to fight them.' I felt for Paula. In order to take down the patriarchy, she had to smile at a man she longed to kill.

The university's logo featured an immaculate winged woman flying high in the blue empyrean. She was wearing a flowing white dress that emphasised her sexy breasts. I'd dreamed of making a career as a scholar, but the dream had lost its appeal. The flawless feminist heroines sculpted by Paula resembled the university's logo: high-flying, white, and trim. There was more messy, human truth in Interregnum Paula: blood-splattered, hacking at her rival, howling in pain. 'Less! Less!' I hissed at the patriarchy, but that battle didn't spark my imagination. It was plugged into the creative-destructive energies of the Maternal line.

◆

While I was still revising my thesis, a developer had bought Anti and Lenny's building and issued eviction notices all round. Lenny found another flat in St Kilda, and Anti moved to a warehouse near her studio in Prahran. We all went on seeing each other, but now we used the phone more to stay in touch. In May,

Benedict moved back to Auckland, enrolled part-time in a social sciences degree, and wrote that he'd abandoned his book. Shaz had started teacher training, and Says Ann played their final gig.

By the end of 1987 I was back in Sydney to stay. We all went on adventuring, changing. We still thought we'd be friends forever, but we also had appetites and ambitions and dreams. Our letters and calls to each other dwindled as our lives swerved and swerved again. Time kept up its Now-Now-Now, and we didn't pay attention to what was going on. We underestimated the pull of the horizon, we didn't spot each other swirling out to sea.

✦

In the last spring of the twentieth century, I spoke on a panel at a writers' festival in Melbourne. Afterwards, I sat at a long table with the other writers, signing copies of my books. As I was preparing to leave, a woman of whom I'd been vaguely aware, waiting to one side, came forward. Court-shoed, skirt-suited, neutral-toned, corporate-bobbed, clock-faced: Amabel.

She'd heard me speak, she said. 'I took the morning off work to come.' She kept a white-knuckled grip on the strap of her shoulder bag and asked if I had time for a coffee. I was tired, and she'd startled me. I couldn't come up with an excuse.

In a nearby cafe she stirred artificial sweetener into her milkless coffee – time pleated to show me Olivia's sturdy wrists. Amabel was wearing an unusual ring. Fashioned from dull grey metal and engraved with a flower, it was at odds with her expensive watch.

We busied ourselves with our coffees and exchanged bits of news. I said I'd lost touch with Melbourne friends, but that, last I'd heard, Anti was living in Hamburg, and Lenny was teaching in upstate New York. Amabel told me that she was at a firm which specialised in mergers and acquisitions. She was still living in Fitzroy, now with her partner, an architect called Kate.

Amabel's voice didn't change when she mentioned Olivia, but it was plain that Olivia was the reason we were here. From the moment I recognised Amabel, I'd assumed that she was out to confront me on Olivia's behalf. My stomach tensed and I set my cup down with a clatter, bracing myself to meet cold rage.

Amabel asked if I knew that Olivia was dead. My hand went to my throat. I heard myself summoning conventional words. I sipped water, gripping my glass.

It had happened two years earlier, Amabel said. Olivia was living in Sydney. 'She went missing while walking in the Blue Mountains. They found her after three days at the bottom of a gorge. It was on the news – I'm surprised you didn't see it.'

'Two years ago I was living in France.'

She asked if Olivia had got in touch with me after moving to Sydney.

'Why would she have? We weren't friends.'

'She'd read your first novel. She used to talk about you, she said she wished she'd got to know you better when you lived in Melbourne.'

Nothing Amabel told me sounded plausible. I said that I hadn't seen Olivia in years.

'It was a long shot.' Amabel's eyes widened. She tilted her head back, got out a hanky – not a tissue, a fine white hanky – and dabbed her eyes.

'I'm so sorry,' I repeated. I drank more water. I couldn't bring myself to touch her hand.

'They say people confide in writers, don't they? It's easier to talk to someone you don't know well.' It wasn't clear if she was referring to Olivia or herself. She sniffed, folded the hanky into a small square, and touched it to her nostrils. 'I hoped Liv might have said something to you that would make sense of it.'

'Of what?'

'She had plenty of experience with solo walking. But she didn't tell anyone where she was heading that day. The weather was good. And the place she came off the track wasn't tricky.'

I took in what she was telling me.

For the third time I said, 'I'm so sorry.' Olivia was

intensely present at that moment, her stuck smile, her woven hair.

'I've talked to her friends and to people she was close to at work. No one's had anything out of the ordinary to say. It was ridiculous to think she might have opened up to you if she was unhappy. Or that you might have seen that she was. But when something like this happens, you can't help looking for answers in the unlikeliest places. Her father, my parents – we were all devastated.'

Olivia had always clashed with her father, Amabel continued. 'It made losing her even worse for him. She blamed him for the divorce, blamed him for everything.' I watched her turn her empty cup a quarter circle on its saucer. I'd never got around to buying bowls for milky coffee, and now that I drank only espressos there was no longer any point.

Amabel was telling me that Olivia had gone into environmental law because her father worked for a mining company. 'Liv took everything to heart. She said that he stole from the earth. She'd started calling him The Thief.'

Keeping my tone light, I asked, 'Was she still with Kit?'

'God, no. That was hopeless, wasn't it? They both met other people after he left Melbourne. He's been out of the picture for years.' Amabel shrugged. 'There was no one special at the time. Liv was caught up in her work. A lot of the outcomes were pretty demoralising, but she felt it was important to keep trying.' She pressed her lips together. 'That's what I used to believe, anyway. Now I'm not sure I ever really knew what she was thinking. I keep going over our conversations. I might have missed something. A sign.'

Amabel didn't offer to pay for my coffee, nor I for hers. At the cash register, her ring caught my eye once again. She saw me looking at it and turned it on her finger, saying, 'It was a present from Liv.'

The street was brisk with lunch-hour workers. Ignoring their pointed sighs, Amabel kept us standing there in the sunny cold as they veered past. Twenty kilos lighter than the last time we'd met, she remained majestic. Staring over my head, she told me that when Olivia and she were still students and living in Fitzroy, she'd gone into Olivia's room one afternoon in search of a book. The room had a balcony, and Olivia was standing there, leaning over the rail. 'I yelled, "Liv!" She turned around but kept one hand on the rail. The way she looked just for a moment – it made me feel afraid.'

She said, 'It was nothing, really.'

She said, 'I think about it every day.'

She needed a story, but I didn't have one to give her. I still hadn't quite taken in her news. All I could come up with to say was that inconsequential things could seem meaningful, could seem weighted with consequence and sense.

I was holding my new book, which didn't fit into my overstuffed bag. Amabel glanced at it. She said, 'I'm afraid I haven't read your work. I've never seen the point of historical novels, to be frank.'

✦

A Canadian writer was interviewed at the festival that evening. He'd begun his career as a journalist, but had recently taken up fiction and produced a global hit. When the interviewer asked why he'd decided to write a novel, the writer replied that he'd been drawn to the 'moral seriousness' of the form. Novels enabled us to look deeply into other people, he said, including those whose lives were very different from ours. The novel was an ethical device for eliciting the reader's empathy and compassion by showing that strangers were really just like us. He spoke with passion and sincerity, and a smattering of applause broke out.

Once, when I was berating my mother for failing to live up to my ambitions, she'd cried, 'You don't know what it's like to be me!' The Woolfmother constructed interiority in radical new ways in her fiction by describing what she found when she looked into herself. That looking inspired her to assemble a feminist politics from her experience of patriarchy: she knew what it was like to be her. But she didn't know what it was like to be E. W. Perera and she didn't care to find out.

He was simply as 'inscrutable' to her as the world from which he came.

I wanted to ask the Canadian writer about characters whose inner lives revealed thinking we disagreed with and even found repellent. Did we summon empathy and compassion for them? If novels presented us with people who turned out to be 'just like us', was that 'moral seriousness' or the comforting reflection of our values and beliefs?

Olivia was tangled up in all this, of course, she was tangled up in everything since I'd learned she was dead. I thought, I'll dream of her tonight; and straight away yielded to something like a dream. Olivia was walking ahead of me on an uneven mountain track. Her plait, grown as fat and coarse as rope, bounced between her shoulder blades, her calves gleamed in the harsh light. It was imperative to catch up with her, so I shouted, 'Liv!' When she turned around, her face was full of wonder. Once again that syllable had saved or condemned her – which?

All those years ago I'd been careful not to see into Olivia, preferring to create an effigy whose capacity for love and suffering and joy fell far short of mine. What was shaming was the certainty that if she'd sought me out in Sydney, I'd have exhumed that effigy. The Canadian reasoned as if the politics of novels were the politics of politics. They were not. What politics asked of us was to care about people we couldn't see into, and the difficulty of that was the difficulty of life.

✦

Social media, the diary form of the new century, arrived. Kit's Facebook cover photo showed terraced paddies rising behind thatched houses and palms. His profile picture was a snow-capped peak. The page was locked, but Google found him for me twice more.

A British newspaper ran a piece about the inhabitants of a township in Madagascar who'd complained about noise from a nearby mine. A photo showed the couple leading the protest. Grim-jawed and lank-haired, clad in lifeless dark garments, they told of sleeplessness, vibrations and migraines, standing their ground in front of a gate that was coming unhinged. Kit, not pictured but identified as the project manager at the mine, was quoted to the effect that Integrity Minerals took the complaints seriously and was working towards resolving the matter. I studied the photo of the couple again. They reminded me of the people in Anti's smudgy drawings: people who waited, people ground small in history's machine.

A West Australian newspaper had a more recent story about a house that was up for an architectural award. The piece was paywalled, but the accompanying photo showed the owners of the house. Blond wood shelves displayed what the caption described as 'eclectic treasures picked up on the couple's extensive travels'. Standing behind a kitchen bench, Kit and his wife, Shirin, looked healthy, contented, and rich. Kit had grown jowls and had horn-rimmed glasses. He was clad in Scandi fawns and whites, like his kitchen and his wife. I wondered if his dealings with women still unfolded as Capture and Take and Shoot. A potted plant flourished beside him, a thick-stemmed, blood-bloomed cactus, thornily erect.

✦

A few years ago, a historian I knew posted a selfie on Facebook. In the background was a multivolume set of books, *The Diaries of Donald Friend*, published by the National Library of Australia between 2001 and 2006. A woman commenting on the post noted that although the Australian artist's diaries were 'illuminating as history', she was astonished that a national institution had published them. She was alluding to the fact that Friend was a paedophile, as his diaries attest.

After an adult relationship in Australia collapsed in 1946, Friend resolved to 'run about the face of the earth' and find himself 'a nice simple black boy'. His theatre of operations included freshly postcolonial Ceylon and freshly postcolonial Bali. In the 1960s, he acquired a magnificent property at Sanur in Bali, where he lived for close to twenty years. Eventually, a combination of ill-health and pressure from the Indonesian authorities drove him home. Barry Humphries, one of the international celebrities who visited Friend in Sanur, writes that in Australia, his 'benevolent form of paedophilia was less favourably regarded'. Friend died in Sydney in 1989 at the age of seventy-four.

A white man's wealth can buy a great many things in a developing country, including impunity from the law. At his property in Sanur, Friend kept a large entourage of 'houseboys' drawn from impoverished Balinese families: young men, adolescents, and children. His diary documents that one of those children entered his household at the age of six. A different child, identified as F., is described as 'an enchanting wayward lover', who goes about sex with Friend 'gaily' and 'enthusiastically'. F. is 'very inventive' and 'not at all sentimental'. Friend continues: 'Clinging and squirming in an embrace he sometimes seizes the radio and holds it to his ear, listening ecstatically to faint far foreign voices, or to jazz and more static, whispering and crooning to the radio and to me turn by turn.'

As tourism to the island escalates, Friend complains of foreign paedophiles corrupting the local boys. By 'corruption' he means that the Balinese now expect payment for sex. A sex tourist asks a local pimp for 'little boys', and F. is procured for him. Friend laments that F. will be 'halfway to prostitution' if he returns.

Sex tourism resembles every other kind of tourism in one iron regard: the tourist unfailingly attracts the pioneer's contempt.

~~'Benevolent' paedophile.~~

~~God.~~

~~Faun~~.

Pig.

Pig!

Pig!

(With apologies to pigs.)

Kerry Negara, an Australian living in Bali, made a documentary called *A Loving Friend* about the artist's Sanur domain. Released in 2009, it can now be viewed online. It includes interviews with four middle-aged Balinese men who knew Friend or belonged to his household. One man, a child at the time he was abused, is angry and ashamed to learn that he's named in the diaries as one of Friend's sexual partners. The artist's Australian friends were offered the opportunity to redact sensitive material about themselves, but no one had tracked down the Balinese man and asked for his consent.

Friend's servants shared information with each other. One man tells Negara that he knew to keep his distance from the artist, especially when Friend, an alcoholic, was drunk. One man says he was worried about his little brother, described as Friend's 'favourite', because he'd been warned that the artist had sex with children. One night Friend told the favourite to go to his room, so his brother sought the assistance of young men from the village. When they arrived at Friend's bedroom door, the artist came out holding a dagger, and the men fled.

Negara interviews the favourite as well. He says that Friend paid for his schooling for six years. He says that if Friend wanted sex and was refused, the refusal was accepted. He says that he didn't have sex with Friend. He says that he never went back to visit the artist after leaving the household. He says he can't remember why. He wonders why he can't remember. He begins to weep.

Negara's Australian interviewees include the founding director of the Australian Music Centre, who retired to Bali. He claims that the Balinese children seduced Friend rather than the other way around. He's met some of Friend's former servants, he says. 'They're not damaged goods.'

Negara also interviews three men whose professional reputations are linked to Friend's: the editor of his diaries, his biographer, and the then head curator of Australian art at the Art Gallery of New South Wales. They, too, defend Friend, denying or making light of his crimes. I thought of the large sign that Humphries tells us hung on Friend's gate in Sanur: No Admission.

The Australian men fascinated me, because, as they

spoke, I heard an echo I couldn't trace to its source. It wasn't until I watched the documentary a third time that the tantalising mist of déjà vu cleared. What I'd recognised was the bluster, evasiveness, and blanking of victims in Prince Andrew's 2019 *Newsnight* interview.

But something genuine gleams through the side-stepping and ducking. It's the faint bemusement in the men's replies. They seem to not quite understand why anyone would think there was a case to answer. Their words reach us from a different world, one in which a child squirming and clinging in a man's bed is of no account. That child is wiser than the men. His imagination is larger than theirs. He seeks comfort in a radio, in the voices and sounds that tell him there are lives beyond the one in which he finds himself trapped. By contrast, the men appear not to recognise any reality larger than their own. They appear not to realise that an invisible audience is assessing their performance:

No Distinction.

No Pass With Merit.

No Pass.

The Balinese villagers who lived near Friend called him *Tuan Rakshasa*: 'Lord Devil'. One of his apologists assured me that it was a term of endearment and respect. 'Tell the truth and shame the devil.' But the devil refuses to be shamed.

✦

Three years into this century, my mother died. It's what mothers do. Daughters tell themselves they've escaped, but that power reverts to mothers at the end. My aunt and I were with my mother when she stepped out of the world. There were three people in the room, one breathed out and then there were two.

As it aged, my mother's body had shrunk everywhere except in the middle. In the last year of her life she'd looked like a pregnant child. In death, her contours annihilated by a heavy quilt, she'd attained the truthfulness of formless form.

A landline was at hand, but my aunt called her husband on her mobile to tell him the news. Then she called each of her sons. I'm talking about a time when not everyone had a mobile phone. My aunt's sequence of practised gestures – taking out her phone, flipping it open, manipulating tiny keys – had the aura of staged events. They were imbued with modernity and magic. They looked like tricks.

The conversation between my aunt and her younger son ran on for quite a while. She'd moved away to the door of the room, but I could hear her talking about his bathroom renovation. Her voice was indulgent and amused as she discussed vanities and taps. Across the street, the last of the sunlight shining in a eucalypt made it appear brighter than any earthly tree. It seemed incredible that my mother had gone where that golden light couldn't follow. 'You better get back to that grouting, love,' I heard my aunt say at last. 'Unless you'd like a word with Cindy? She's right here.'

My mother was cremated. Seventeen years earlier, I'd cremated the Woolfmother, too. The last thing I did before leaving my flat in St Kilda was set a match to her in the sink. I watched steadily as she curled and blackened under the flame. When it was all over, I turned on the tap and washed away her remains.

I donated some of my mother's possessions to a charity and threw away the rest. Her furniture included a standard lamp acquired secondhand while I was still at school. The shade was made of a rosy, taffeta-like fabric fashioned into ridges and valleys. Edged with satin and embroidered braid, it resembled the fluted skirt of a dress a little girl might wear to a party – it even had a wired cambric hoop underneath, a stiff petticoat to give it volume and make it flare.

The shade struck me as the delayed fulfilment of a wish. It stood in for all the expensive, yearned-for clothes that my mother hadn't had as a child. When she married well and had a child of her own, she put me in frilly party frocks with sticking-out skirts, frocks coloured the lemon, pale blue, mauve or rose of birthday-cake icing – I'd loathed them, of course. At party time, I'd weep and plead. 'What kind of little girl doesn't like pretty dresses?' my mother would ask, bewildered. At the last minute, with the charity's van drawing up outside my mother's building, I wavered. The pink-shaded lamp had brought my mother joy. I decided to keep it for myself.

The lamp clashed with my efficient, modern furniture and would have embarrassed me in a public room. I placed it in a corner of my study. The wiring was faulty, so I never plugged it in, and after a while I stopped noticing it. Years went by, and a journalist arrived to interview me. While we were talking in my study, her gaze kept drifting to a point beyond my shoulder and a look of astonishment would pass over her face. Finally I asked what was distracting her. She apologised. 'It's that lamp,' she said. 'I hope you don't mind me saying it's really ugly.'

I was taken aback at first. But then I realised it was only right that a young woman should look at decorative pink femininity without nostalgia or desire. I remembered my detested party dresses with their hard net petticoats that made me itch. Adults seeing me in those dresses unfailingly said I looked sweet. My mother and the Woolfmother were fastened into that sugary vision of femaleness at birth. When they were grown, they both found themselves negotiating lives for which nothing had prepared them. One was a brilliant writer, and the other called magazines books, and between them they passed on a lot of information I've needed. It's not that I put them on my head and walk, but you could say they helped build my brain.

The last time I examined the lampshade it was dust-grimed, moth-holed and askew on its base. Symbol and repository of dumb, mixed feelings, it persists where I see/don't see it every day.

I've never stopped expecting my mother to call me. Sometimes a kind mirror shows me her face. I find myself thinking back through her, just as the Woolfmother predicted I would. Take the day when the training wheels came off my daughter's bike and, Thrilled to the Marrow, she set out to ride the length of the park. 'Go, go, *go*!' I shouted, but inside I was screaming, You will break all your teeth.

My mother believed that the devil is attracted to spilled salt. She said that whenever I spilled some, a pinch thrown over my left shoulder would keep the devil at bay. It's advice I've passed on to my daughter. It didn't always work for me, but I want her to have all the luck she can get.

✦

Last July I went to London for a gathering of Commonwealth writers and scholars held in an imposing eighteenth-century house. It had been built for a man who amassed a fortune from his plantations in the Caribbean. Later in life he campaigned for abolition and poor relief, and was now honoured as a philanthropist. A poet from Ghana remarked that the whole set-up, including the conference, perfectly illustrated an observation in V. S. Naipaul's *A Bend in the River*: 'The Europeans wanted gold and slaves, like everybody else; but at the same time they wanted statues put up to themselves as people who had done good things for the slaves.'

Readings were to be held each evening after dinner, to which end we writers were divided into groups. An assortment of mahogany dining chairs and stackable plastic ones were arranged in semicircles in what had once been a drawing room. It had a magnificent fireplace with a tall mirror above it, a chandelier like a brass spider, and carpet that looked as if it had been chosen to stand up to wear.

My group was to read on the second evening, so on the first I sat in the audience. One by one, three writers read from their latest work, each for their allotted ten minutes. Then the last writer rose to take her place under the spider. She came from an island where she was deeply admired but was little known elsewhere. Over the course of a long career she'd published many books, but she was carrying a sheaf of papers and announced that on this, her first visit to England, she was going to read something written for the occasion.

She began by drawing our attention to the discrepancy between her English name and her un-English appearance. Her ancestry was 'a confluence of imperial desires', she said. There followed an account of her early childhood, which coincided with the Second World War. She wrote vividly, and the subject was gripping. Her country had suffered greatly in the conflict, in which it had played a heroic part.

By this time her ten minutes were up, but she continued unabashed. She was an old woman, and it soon became apparent that she intended to recount the story of her life. For a period she'd been involved in politics, and she railed against ministerial corruption and the injustices various governments had inflicted on her fellow citizens. It wasn't always easy to follow the ins-and-outs of those bygone intrigues. In addition, her piece seemed to have been written with increasing haste and no revision, because it grew repetitive, lost its thread, looped back and forth. All the while her voice remained grave and unhurried. She held herself very straight, and unlike the rest of us she was formally attired, in a dark dress and a fuchsia jacket with a jewelled brooch.

Darkness gathered in the floor-length windows behind her. It had been a long day of papers and discussions, many of us were jet-lagged, and we'd all eaten a substantial meal. Eyelids drooped. Someone emitted a trill of soft little snores. But I saw people listening carefully as well. A woman who was the by-product of an empire had finally travelled to its centre to tell us about matters of importance in her world. She'd been admitted to a drawing room and invited to speak. But what power has a voice that isn't heard and respected? We offered her the justice of attending to her words.

✦

The conference ended, and I went to Paris, where my daughter would be joining me in a couple of days. I called her in Trieste, where she was visiting her father's family, and we talked for a while. Afterwards I went out for a walk. Earlier the heat and the glare had been stunning, but the evening was silky. The cafe terraces were crowded with diners and people waiting for tables, making it awkward to pick my way past.

Lights were starting to come on in apartments. I was studying the window display in a bookshop called Comme Un Roman when an SUV pulled up at the curb. A man and two little girls climbed out, and the woman at the wheel drove away. As soon as the smaller child realised that her mother had left, she began to roar. 'I want my mummy!' she howled, and instant rivers rolled down her cheeks. Her father tried to comfort her, saying that her mother would be back before bedtime. What use was that to the child? Her loss at that moment was absolute and pure.

I went on, turned a corner, and saw the Cirque d'Hiver at the far end of the street. The winter circus, that curved golden building with a sequins-and-ice name, never seemed wholly of this world. Set in the deepening blue of a summer evening, it could have been a dream of itself.

A thickset man was making his way towards me on foot. Lenny and I recognised each other at the same time. It sounds like a novel, doesn't it, *comme un roman*. But Paris is a novelistic place. It lends itself to walking, which conjures encounters and ghosts. Lenny's hair was white but still lavish and curly. He looked like his own ancestor, and no doubt I looked the same. We clung to each other like swimmers in trouble. It felt as if this meeting had always been waiting for us, trapped in time and finally released.

I suggested a drink in a cafe I knew near the Cirque d'Hiver. Lenny replied that he wasn't keen on cafes these days. He lived nearby, he said, and invited me to dinner in his apartment instead. As we walked, I learned that Lenny had been living in Paris for years. He'd left academia and now ran a gallery that specialised in outsider art. His French husband, a cinematographer, was in Slovenia for work, and Lenny would be joining him when the gallery closed for the August break. He remarked on my books in his kindly way. I told him about Anti, restored to me by Instagram. I told him a few things about my life.

In Lenny's apartment I looked out at the moon idling above treetops and roofs. Lights shone in every building now. It was that strange summer hour when reality slips. The luminous cobalt sky was still anchored in evening, but the moon, the glowing windows and the dark, massy foliage had crossed into night. The eye and the brain, shuttling from one to the other, found nothing to trust.

Lenny was opening foil packets and jars, filling bowls with snacks. He fetched champagne from the fridge. I asked why he avoided cafes – was he put off by the summer crowds? Lenny's busy hands went still. He'd been caught up in the 2015 terrorist attacks, he said. A friend he'd been dining with at one of the cafes sprayed with gunfire was killed. Another friend was shot in the spine and now lived in a blur of medication and pain. 'I was lucky – the bullet only grazed me here.' He shifted a lock of his hair. I saw the white scar on his red face.

Yet another of Lenny's friends escaped injury, but recently his wife had left him. The events of that November evening had come to dominate his life. He joined Facebook groups, vanished down internet rabbit holes, travelled across France and beyond to meet with survivors and the bereaved. Crises in his family erupted and subsided unnoticed by him. During the interminable trial of the sole terrorist who survived, he attended court every day. He wrote to the prisoner, letters that received no response and contained romantic words like 'soldier' and 'forgiveness' and 'spring'. His wife believed that over many years of working as an editor in a publishing house, he'd come to confuse realism with reality. It was her opinion that he was looking to life for the satisfactions provided by novels: the possibility of redemption, answers and patterns, motive and cause. Women were mocked for Bovarysme, but in her experience it was men who were swayed by well-worn narrative tropes. Life was random and cruel, she said, and she'd lost patience with his unwillingness to face that fact.

Lenny twisted the cork from the bottle – expertly, without a pop. He handed me my glass and raised his in a toast: 'Well, we have come this far.' It was the last line of Bishop's 'Cirque d'Hiver'. But all that was the past.

ACKNOWLEDGEMENTS

Thank you, thank you, thank you:

Michael Heyward and all at Text, especially W. H. Chong and Emma Schwarcz;

Nat Jansz, Mark Ellingham, and all at Sort of Books;

Kendall Storey and all at Catapult, especially John McGhee;

Debra Adelaide, Saskia Beudel, Emily Bitto, Bernadette Brennan, Wenona Byrne, Mridula Chakraborty, Sophie Cunningham, Clare Drysdale, Martin Edmond, Roanna Gonsalves, Zahia Hafs, Sarah Holland-Batt, Mireille Juchau, Mayu Kanamori, Malcolm Knox, Joy Lai, Jen Livett, Liz McMahon, Myles Neri, Kate Nossal, Brigitta Olubas, Felicity Plunkett, Josephine Rowe, Carrie Tiffany;

Sara White for information about music exams;

Walter Perera for information about his great-uncle, E. W. Perera;

Fiona McFarlane and Neel Mukherjee for reading the manuscript and offering wise counsel;

beloved Sarah Lutyens;

beloved Chris Andrews.

Excerpt from *Spring* by Ali Smith. Copyright © 2019 by Ali Smith. Reprinted by kind permission of Ali Smith.

Excerpt from 'The Ideal' from *Out of Danger* by James Fenton. Copyright © 1994 by James Fenton. Reprinted by permission of Farrar, Strauss and Giroux.

Excerpt from 'Cirque d'Hiver' from *Poems* by Elizabeth Bishop. Copyright © 2011 by The Alice H. Methfessel Trust. Publisher's Note and compilation copyright © 2011 by Farrar, Straus and Giroux. Reprinted by permission of Farrar, Straus and Giroux.

© Joy Lai

MICHELLE DE KRETSER was born in Sri Lanka. She lives in Warrane/Sydney on unceded Gadigal land. An honorary associate of the English department at the University of Sydney, she has won several awards for her fiction. *Theory & Practice* is her seventh novel.